LUPO

AND THE SECRET OF WINDSOR CASTLE

Look out for

Lupo and the Curse at Buckingham Palace

THE ADVENTURES of a ROYAL DOG

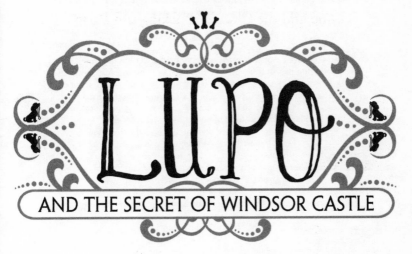

LUPO

AND THE SECRET OF WINDSOR CASTLE

ABY KING

Illustrated by Sam Usher

Hodder
Children's
Books

A division of Hachette Children's Books

Hodder Children's Books
a division of Hachette Children's Books
338 Euston Road, London NW1 3BH
An Hachette UK company

www.hachette.co.uk
www.theadventuresoflupo.com

For Lilly and Malte

And my godchildren who constantly
inspire me:

Sienna De Gale,

Lilly Titchener-Barrett,

Freddie and Arabella Field,

Henry Cullis.

Contents

The Duke made sure that everyone was ready. Prince George was sitting up in his cot wide awake. The Duchess smoothed down a tuft of unruly blond baby hair. Then she tucked her young son into the softest royal blankets.

It was time for tonight's bedtime story. Someone turned on the baby light, filling the blue room with a comforting warm glow.

Under the cot, Lupo stretched out his big black paws, breathing in the heavenly smell of bath bubbles and baby powder. He smiled to himself, picturing Nanny's angry face at the sight of him playing with Prince George in the bath tonight. She hadn't been pleased they were playing "bubble crown".

Nanny had turned her back for but a moment to

get a new bar of soap, leaving Lupo unguarded. The Prince was purposely sitting on the old bar of soap. He burbled, in his own special way, *"Errrrpluff!"* which roughly translated means, "Quick get in! Let's play BUBBLE CROWN!"

Lupo obeyed and took flight, but instead of gracefully leaping on to the bath he managed to flop headfirst into the warm water. Soapy bubbles scattered into the air and covered the bathroom floor.

By the time Nanny finished rummaging in the bathroom cabinet George had won! He had the biggest crown of bubbles. Lupo's medium-sized crown was sliding off his wet dangling ear. She shook her fists and waggled her fat fingers, flabbergasted.

"GET OUT, LUPO! What on earth are you two up to? I turn my back for a second and you . . . I—" cried Nanny, as she frogmarched him out of the bath.

Not even the Duke and Duchess understood that the strange *Gurgles* and *Sniffs* muttered by their son and spaniel were actually a secret language.

Lupo and George shared such a strong bond that they were able to talk to one another. Only a handful of children throughout history have been able to understand their pets. Lupo wasn't sure when he realized he could talk to George or that the Prince could talk back. It just happened one day and they understood each other perfectly.

As he left the bathroom, still covered in bubbles, he *barked* back to George, "I will win next time, your Royal Highness!" His wet paw prints led all the way down the corridor and into the nursery.

Lupo smiled to himself once more. Tonight had been fun. Licking his front paw, he noticed a few small bubbles still hung on his damp black fur.

The Duke settled into a chair in the nursery and opened his book.

"This is the story of a great knight," he said, and at once Lupo's shaggy black tail wagged with excitement. "His name was George and it's about how he had to fight a nasty horrible dragon."

Lupo's ears pricked. This was going to be a good book. When Lupo spoke to the Prince, he looked straight into George's eyes. What sounded like sniffs and lip smacking to the Duke and Duchess was actually Lupo speaking.

Sniff!, then a loud *chomp*, followed lastly by a series of *licks* represented, "Dragons, George! Did you hear that, we've got monsters tonight – this might be the best story ever." His tail bumped against the wooden cot, a sign of utter happiness. *Thump, thump, thump*.

"Dragons! Woohoo!" replied George happily with a long burble.

The Duke looked up from the book, convinced he had just heard his son mutter his first word! But he brushed away the thought, reminding himself that George was far too young to be talking. Mumbles and gurgles were nothing more than that. Lupo, of course, knew better.

Clearing his throat, the Duke began, "Once upon a time there was a young farm boy called George. He was short and not very strong. He had long, thin legs and spindly arms. His hair was a mop of brilliant red and he was covered from head to toe in freckles . . . just like my brother!"

"That is not how the story begins," said the Duchess, picking up a wet towel from the floor. She smiled at the sight of her family all ready for bed. "If I remember, this story begins with a dragon – a great big dragon, roaring through the countryside!"

Prince George began jumping up and down against the front of the cot. "*Chuff . . . Dodo . . .*

chuff!" (Roar . . . Lupo . . . roar!)

Taking in a big gulp of air, Lupo opened his throat and roared as loudly as he could – roaring was something everyone could understand.

"More, more, roar, more!" George begged Lupo in excited mumbles.

"ROOOAARRRRRR!" bellowed the Duke, joining in.

George giggled loudly.

The Duchess bent down and patted Lupo's head. "Lupo, stop encouraging them. That is quite enough! Anyone would think I have a zoo in this nursery. That means you too!" she chided her unruly husband.

George looked at Lupo wide-eyed, and smiled a big toothless grin. Bedtime stories with the Duke were much better than with boring Nanny.

The Duke turned the book so that everyone could see the front page. "Pretty big dragon, don't you think?" he said.

A picture of a dragon filled the first page with flames of red and gold. Lupo couldn't help but *bark*. He had never seen anything like it. George was captivated and fell as silent as a kitchen mouse.

5

The Duke continued reading: "England was under attack from a fearsome dragon. It had long, twisted claws and ragged wings, skin as cold as snakes and yellow eyes which lured its prey into a vice-like grip of death.

"The King of England was desperate. He had sent many soldiers to try and slay the dragon. All of them had failed. The King asked his court despairingly, 'Send a message to every village that I am willing to offer my daughter's hand in marriage to anyone who can rid this land of the terrible beast!'

"News of the reward spread far. The Princess was the most beautiful woman in England, so many young men took up their swords, hoping to win her hand in marriage. They all tried but none could kill the loathsome dragon.

"Deep in the middle of the countryside lived a simple farmer called George. He had not been trained to be a warrior or a skilled knight. One day, as he worked in the fields, he had a vision that he could slay the dragon and marry the beautiful Princess. He wasted no time and left his farm and rode to the city, offering himself as a servant to the King.

"When George saw how scared the Princess

was, he promised her that he would rid the land of the dragon."

Suddenly, there was a tap-tap-tap on the glass of the nursery window. Jumping out from under the cot, Lupo grumbled, "It's here, George, it's the dragon!"

George waved frantically in the direction of the nursery window.

Stooping low to the floor, like a lion preparing to catch its prey, Lupo went to investigate. Staring into the darkness of the royal garden, he saw it was a heavy tree branch swinging in the rain, casting eerie shadows.

His racing heart calmed, and he woofed, "It's just rain, but let's pretend it was the dragon!"

George stared out the window in astonishment. Then he tried to climb out of his cot to see the dragon at the window. The Duchess caught him as he tumbled forward. He grabbled at his mummy's pink jumper.

Ignoring the commotion, the Duke carried on reading: "Determined to save the kingdom, brave George rode into the mountains towards the dragon's cave."

Lupo squeezed between the Duchess's feet, looking up at George who was dribbling all over her jumper. "*Whoof! Grrr, growl.*" (George, we have to get to the dragon's cave.)

"*Reeeee!*" (There, I can see it!) George's chubby little arms shook at the wardrobe.

"The day turned to night as George grew close to the lair," the Duke went on. "Thick black smoke filled the air together with the smell of rotten eggs . . ."

Lupo snorted a deep *p-woof*. "Rotten eggs! George, that's nasty," he said, jumping up and down. He stuck his wet, black nose into the pages of the book. But it was no good. He couldn't detect the dragon's scent.

George quivered. The dragon smelt like his nappy! Then he and Lupo both fell into fits of giggles.

"George had arrived at the entrance to the dragon's cave . . ."

Thunder stole everyone's attention. The dark room flickered brightly as lightning streaked the night sky. Lupo gripped the carpet with his paws. He growled at the pages of the book, knowing that any minute, George the knight would be face-to-face with the dragon.

"George aimed his sword and raced into the darkness on his horse. Fire surrounded him. The dragon glared at him ready to destroy him like so many others.

"George charged towards the dragon and struck the wretched creature with a hard blow. Shocked, it fell backwards and tried to steady itself. It was very angry! The dragon then reared on to its hind legs and flapped its long wings. From its mouth it blew orange fire all around George and his horse.

"George was too quick. In seconds he was underneath it. With one large surge he forced his sword into the heart of the dragon, bringing it crashing to the ground. The dragon was dead.

"Returning to the palace, the King and Queen were so happy they made George a Knight of the Realm."

Noticing that both his son and the dog were not settling down to sleep, the Duke shut the book. "Enough adventures for tonight. It's bedtime for you both. Come on now, settle down."

"He didn't read about the Princess and the marriage and England finally being safe," booed George. He was sad that the story was finished.

9

Lupo clambered on to the side of the cot and, sticking his black face in between the wooden bars, licked George's pink hands. He said, "George, you did it – you saved the Princess!"

The exhausted prince *gaahed*, "I did?"

"Yes, you did!" woofed Lupo.

"We did it together, Lupo!" burbled the royal baby.

And then with a sniff and a woof, Lupo crawled into his bed. He had to turn several times to get into the most comfortable position. "Yes we did. Night night, buddy."

George wasn't quite ready for bed. "*Raar!*" he cried. "Yippee, that was the best book . . . AGAIN!"

The Duchess bent down to both her son and dog and said, "Sleep well, you two. No more thoughts of St George and the dragon. Night, night."

Prince George began to moan as his parents left the room, pulling the door to.

Lupo tried to comfort him. He lay on his back and put a warm paw on the underside of the Prince's cot, "Don't be upset, George. I'm right here."

The gentle sound of Lupo's voice instantly made him feel better. The Prince mumbled sleepily,

"Lupo, if we are asleep, how will we know if the dragon is coming?"

Lupo's eyelids felt very heavy, "I'll smell him . . . rotten eggs remember . . ." Closing his eyes, he fell into a deep sleep.

George snuggled against his toy wombat and also went to sleep.

But the happy evening in the nursery was soon spoilt by a strange dream. As Lupo slept, he dreamt he was cold and alone in a very dark place. Suddenly there was a large white swan. It was injured.

"An accident perhaps," thought Lupo. The bird then spoke these words to him: "Protect the secret." Somewhere, a dog barked. It was a scary kind of bark.

Lupo thrashed around under the cot, his nose twitched left and right. He caught the scent of something . . . the smell of rotten eggs.

Next, a huge dragon appeared. With its sharp claws and gnashing teeth, it roared so loudly it woke him up.

Lupo sat up stiffly and checked on George. He was happy to see the prince was sucking his thumb blissfully.

He went to the Duke and Duchess's room and hopped onto their bed. He lay at their feet as they slept but he was unable to sleep. Instead his thoughts were filled with images of the dragon from the story.

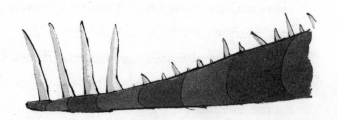

1
Humble Beginnings

Lupo was a very young puppy when he spent his first night with the royal couple at their cottage by the sea in Wales. He howled as loudly as he could, even though he had the nicest of beds and a belly full of warm milk.

His wolfish cries for attention had kept the Duke and Duchess awake all night. They had tried to teach him to sleep in his own bed but just as the skies turned pink and dawn's first light appeared on the horizon, the Duke had given in and come and rescued Lupo from his misery. He was scooped up and given a cozy spot right in the middle of their bed. Comforted by their presence he felt like he was where he belonged.

The sleepy Duke had mumbled his name for the

first time that night. "Lupo," he said, mid yawn. "It means *wolf* in Italian."

"Yes," the Duchess had replied. "Yes . . . he is our little wolf!"

Lupo was a black ball of shaggy fur, all ears and podgy paws when he'd first come to Anglesey. He had no idea he was a royal dog, no understanding of what it meant to be royalty.

The small cottage was the perfect place to be a puppy. He would spend his days digging around in the Duchess's handbag for buried treasure or hide in the bottom of the Duke's helicopter bags marked HRH. There was all sorts of trouble to be had – he could destroy high heels or bury car keys in the vegetable patch, though for some reason no one was very happy with his muddy paw prints or the chewed-up leather shoes scattered on the living room carpet.

Back then they would go on long walks. When it was time to leave the Duke and Duchess would pull on big rubber wellies and go down to the beach to skim pebbles on the crashing waves. Lupo loved chasing crabs as they tried to escape him, running sideways down the beach.

His sleek black coat was often wet and windswept from jumping in and out of rock pools. Afterwards, he would lie in the summer sunshine, his eyes growing heavy as patches of his coat dried in the warm beams. His long ears gently fluttered in the sea breeze as he listened to the cottage mice busily foraging in the grasses around him. The mice were his friends and at the end of long happy days Lupo liked nothing more than to watch them as they danced around the tiny living room.

The happy royal couple spoilt him rotten! He'd snuggle between them on the sofa as they talked and laughed together. He woke them up every morning just so they would make him a breakfast of fresh scrambled eggs or warm porridge!

But he wasn't a puppy any more. He was at Kensington Palace, far from his humble beginnings by the sea.

Lupo had made himself comfortable on the top of the Duke and Duchess's duvet. As he lay in the dark, he watched as the palace ghosts of Queen Mary II and King William III poked their heads around the bedroom door. They didn't say anything. The Queen smiled at him. He pushed the strange dream out of his thoughts and focused on trying to go back to sleep. He tried to imagine himself in the grass at the little cottage and the time filled with sunshine and sea swells.

Finally he drifted back to sleep, the dragon was gone . . . for now.

The move to London had not been easy. Leaving behind the cottage was sad but necessary. It was time for Lupo to grow up and become the royal dog the nation expected. Their new home would be Kensington Palace. Lupo would be sharing it with a royal baby.

When the Duchess had found out she was expecting Prince George, it seemed the entire world wanted to congratulate them. Flowers, toys and teddy bears filled every room of the pretty cottage. A card sat in the middle of the mat. It was from the Queen. The Duchess said that they had all been invited to London to have a celebration tea at Buckingham Palace.

"I think it's high time for you to meet the other royal dogs," said the Duke, ruffling the top of Lupo's head. He turned to his wife and said, "Let's take him with us – it's time he got to know London, anyway. It won't be long before Kensington Palace is ready and until then he'll have a huge palace to get used to."

The following day, as the royal car drove through London, Lupo sat in his navy blue bed, utterly gobsmacked. The city was buzzing! He could hear the hustle and bustle of busy people. Traffic raced past the car's windows.

He barked at a multicoloured symphony of umbrellas outside a tube station and he felt his heart bouncing against his chest in excitement.

"Wow," he said under his breath, hoping that no one could hear him, as they drove around Hyde Park Corner. "An angel with horses . . ."

As the car stopped at a set of traffic lights, he jumped up to get a better look around. To the left of him there were huge black and gold gates leading into Green Park. Ahead he could see Big Ben. Someway in the distance was the London Eye and *there* was Nelson's Column!

The car began turning right. Queen Victoria sat in all her glory at the entrance to Buckingham Palace. Four lions lay quietly at her feet, unmoving.

They were watching – their marble eyes followed Lupo as he bounced around the boot.

"Hello! I'm Lupo!" he shouted, gazing all around. None of the magnificent lions stirred. They were too busy guarding Queen Victoria and her palace.

A crowd of tourists moved towards the car. Someone shouted, "It's them! It's the Duke and Duchess!" A camera flashed. Someone took his picture! The great Buckingham Palace gates closed behind the car and it crunched on to the gravel and rolled beneath a stone archway.

As the royal car came to a stop the Duke said, "We're here, Lupo. No piddling on Granny's carpet! And play nicely with the other dogs. No chewing *anything*, or we shall not be invited back."

Two footmen in brilliant red and gold tailcoats stood either side of the entrance. As Lupo passed them, he saw his own reflection in their highly-polished black shoes.

"Your Royal Highness, may I take Lupo for a walk around the gardens with the other dogs?" offered Tommy the footman.

The Duke looked down at Lupo. "Good idea. Why don't you go with Tommy?"

Nervously scratching his ear, Lupo looked up at the Duke and then at Tommy. The idea of being in the palace was scary enough, but to be left with a stranger felt even worse, but the Duke seemed confident so Lupo slowly began wagging his tail.

"Go and see if you can catch one of those pesky squirrels!" said the Duchess.

Lupo watched as they disappeared. Now he was desperate to go and explore. Buckingham Palace was full of winding staircases, smart corridors and large doors that probably led to priceless trinkets and treasures.

Tommy tugged on his lead as they headed towards the conservatory. He sniffed the clean carpets as they walked and in the air he could smell flowers.

There were no dogs around. He couldn't help but wonder if the famous royal dogs were off having fun somewhere in one of the rooms around him.

Tommy unclicked the lead and Lupo ran into the grand palace gardens. There was a large lake, and the water looked inviting. Lupo loved to swim. Briefly, he considered jumping in but was interrupted by one of the most beautiful dogs he had ever seen: Holly, the Queen's corgi. For a few seconds he totally forgot where he was.

After what seemed like an embarrassingly long pause he finally spoke, trying to be as respectful as possible. "Hello, I'm Lupo, Your Royal Highness."

She responded quickly, rattling off a series of remarks. "It's just Holly – I don't get a title. It's a real pleasure to meet you, Lupo. All the Queen's dogs are looking forward to getting to know you. I hear the servants talking about you *all* the time – you're quite famous in these parts!" She realized she was talking very quickly so stopped and looked down at the freshly-cut grass. She took a deep breath to compose herself.

"It's a real pleasure to meet *you*, Holly," said Lupo. "I've been looking forward to coming to Buckingham Palace. We don't have servants at the cottage, but if we did I am sure they would talk endlessly about this place. I bet you have all kinds of adventures here."

Lupo couldn't help but stare deeply into her eyes which had a way of filling him with warmth. He pulled his gaze away, trying to behave more appropriately. This was one of the Queen's dogs! "How many corgis does Her Majesty have?"

"The Queen has two corgis," Holly replied. "Myself and Willow. But Willow is off resting in the yellow bedroom – she overdid it last night – and has asked me to send her apologies for not being here to welcome you. She likes to stay at Her Majesty's side no matter how late it gets and last night was a late one."

Holly was keen to make Lupo feel as welcome as possible. He was a very good-looking dog, with his long ears, brown eyes and jet black coat. "Were you about to jump in the lake?" she asked.

Lupo felt like he could talk to Holly about anything. "Yes, I was thinking about it. I don't think I have ever seen such an inviting lake. I love swimming. Especially on such a nice day like this. If I lived here I would be in this lake every day!"

"I always wondered what it would be like to go for a swim in there," Holly said. "I'm not a great swimmer, though – legs too short, see!" She looked down at her little legs and lifted a well-manicured paw for him to inspect. "Corgis aren't water dogs like spaniels. We prefer to roll in the grass on days like today! But I did hear a story once about that lake. Apparently it's filled with all kinds of fish.

Vulcan says it's very old, and it used to be a river."
She felt like she was rambling again. "I'm sorry I'm
talking too much."

Lupo shook his head. "No, not at all, I love
history, especially royal history. Who is Vulcan, by
the way?"

Holly pointed. "That's Vulcan. Her Majesty also
has dorgis – they are a cross between a dachshund
and corgi – Candy and Vulcan. Candy is with the
Duke's father in the living room. Vulcan is often
sulking around outside. Come on, I'll introduce
you."

Vulcan was standing under the largest of oak
trees. His beady eyes were fixed firmly on Lupo.

Lupo couldn't help but feel something wasn't
quite right. He noticed the dorgi was keeping his
distance deliberately. He was watching them and it
wasn't in a good way. He was sure he could feel
the strange dog's eyes studying his every move.

Vulcan hadn't taken news of Lupo's visit to
Buckingham Palace well. At the mere mention of the
cocker spaniel's name, Vulcan had felt the hairs on
his coat bristle uncomfortably. His oversized ears

twitched and his short, tidy whiskers flicked back, making him look quite villainous.

He didn't like competing for Her Majesty's attention and, with the new royal baby and Lupo, the public's affections were being stretched in one direction too many. Vulcan was never mentioned on the news or Radio Four. He had to face facts: he no longer registered on the nation's radar.

The Buckingham Palace mice had gathered in corners, saying in hushed tones that Lupo was the future of the monarchy "*a common animal to unite the nation*".

"Rubbish" had been Vulcan's response to that particular comment before breaking the pack up. He had been furious that yet another member of the family had broken with tradition and chosen a breed other than corgis. The royal corgis' blood line was thin enough already. It was in danger of becoming extinct so the fact that the young royal couple had chosen a very common cocker spaniel outraged him. Worse than that, Lupo had no royal pedigree.

Holly used her history lessons to show off. "Queen Victoria had a spaniel called Dash, oh how she loved her. I expect the Duchess feels the same way about Lupo. I bet he will be quite looking forward to meeting us. Bertie tells me . . ."

"Oh please, Holly, whatever next, *greyhounds*? Enough."

The truth was, Vulcan's blood boiled with envy. No one saw that he was the future of the monarchy. Only he had the power to do what needed to be done. Not some common dog.

Holly had betrayed him. She was totally overexcited hearing that the Duke and Duchess would be coming for tea.

Vulcan poured out his cold heart trying to dampen her enthusiasm. "They had better not be bringing that awful cocker spaniel into my palace. Lopo, is it? I mean, *really*, what kind of a name is that for a dog?"

Holly ignored his sneers, "Vulcan, it's *Lupo*, not Lopo! I think it is terrific news!"

"What? That dog will not be around for long if I have anything to do with it. I suggest *you* keep your distance. Whilst we are on the subject you are to stop holding court with Bertie – he's a mouse. It's beneath you."

"Well, Bertie is my friend and he tells me that

Lupo has a way with all kinds of animals. All the mice in the cottage think he is really friendly. I hope he likes *us*. Vulcan, you will try to be welcoming, won't you?" she pleaded. Her pretty smile did nothing to warm his frozen heart.

Vulcan watched as Lupo and Holly headed towards him – here, in *his* garden.

Vulcan deliberately summoned enough anger to ensure that his introduction was less of a welcome and more of a warning. He wanted to send Lupo running as fast as he could back to the little cottage by the sea.

Lupo bowed lowly to Vulcan. Vulcan didn't return the generous gesture. "Lopo, is it?" he asked pointedly, his eyebrows twitching aggressively.

"It's Lupo, and it's a great honour to meet you. I have just been talking to Holly and she tells me that you are—"

Vulcan stared right through him. He interrupted, curtly, "Lopo, Lupo. All the same . . ." The dorgi's mouth curled at the edges – he was happy to have the dog on the back paw already. "I am sure you are all settled into life with the Duke and Duchess.

If I were you, I wouldn't get too comfortable. They will be making changes soon enough and I suspect children will mean that you will be returned to the farm. Children and dogs . . . bad mix."

Lupo was surprised at the most unpleasant of welcomes he had just received. He chose not to reply. Holly was blushing with embarrassment. Vulcan finished, clearly pleased with the reaction on Lupo's mystified black face and ignoring Holly's obvious horror.

"Goodbye, Lopo," said Vulcan, keen to get back to his plotting.

The Queen and the rest of the royal family were heading out to inspect the new roses. Holly suggested that they all head over to meet Candy.

As Lupo walked with Holly he could have sworn he heard Vulcan growling.

2
Kensington Palace

Since Prince George's birth, the family lived in Apartment 1A of Kensington Palace, which was welcoming and comfortable. It was modern and yet traditional. Alongside priceless artworks from the royal collection, there were black and white photographs of precious moments of family life captured by the Duchess. There were a few of Lupo as a puppy enjoying the long Welsh beaches they had left behind.

The young royal couple gave Lupo a nice bed in the palace kitchen. But he never used it. The nursery was where he slept, right beneath baby George.

The royal family shared their new home with other members of the royal family, Nanny and a small group of servants. There was a large part of the palace, which was out of bounds, since it was open to the public. Thousands of tourists came to visit every day.

At first, Lupo had kept within the private part of the palace, but as he got older he found himself yearning to explore the many corridors and rooms that were closed to him. Just after his first birthday he bravely took his first steps beyond the apartment, and headed off to explore his new, enormous palace.

There were plenty of rooms to look into and every one of them was filled with something interesting and new. The public areas were the best places to play – maybe it was because he wasn't allowed in them! He would stick his neck into cupboards, bang his long black tail on priceless sofas, sniff dusty old oil portraits of kings and queens and dig out lunch boxes from visiting children's rucksacks.

Of course the palace staff would find him and often they would struggle to take a half-demolished packed lunch from him.

His new royal home was far grander and quite a bit bigger than the cottage. All sorts of animal families called the important palace their home. Mice, bats, small birds and a wealth of insects crept, crawled, buried and flew in and around the building.

They were different from the animals he had known at the cottage. Kensington Palace's animals all seemed to be so busy! Lupo wished he knew what they all did. The mice, for instance, would run here, there and everywhere carrying bits of paper, wood, fabric and food. Lupo wondered where it all ended up. He thought that they must all go outside, through the tall iron gates and into the perfectly maintained Kensington Gardens. Perhaps they ventured further beyond the gardens and into Hyde Park.

He didn't see himself as a royal dog. He never thought he was above anyone, unlike Vulcan. He would leave the other animals scraps of sandwiches or broken bags of crisps under the main staircase. He'd give rides to smaller insects. They seemed to love hanging off his coat and visiting Prince George. Birds and bats would swoop down to wish him well and he in turn would warn them when Kitty was on the prowl.

Kitty was the palace cat – a tabby, who had no official owners. She had arrived on the back of a milk float as a tiny kitten and had been adopted by the cooks, then the rest of the staff, and pretty soon the other members of the royal family residing in the various apartments.

At first she kept her distance, preferring to wander the long hallways and empty grand staircases alone, but as Lupo grew from a puppy into a young dog he noticed that she started to take more of an interest in him and soon they became friends, even though the first thing she had said to him was, "Cats and dogs can't be friends . . ."

"But why not?" Lupo had replied, confused and innocently questioning the tabby's reasons.

Kitty had looked perplexed. "You know, I never understood why. It's a good question. Leave it with me." She purred as she thought.

For days she considered why cats and dogs could not be friends.

As the days passed, Lupo would patiently ask her the same question, "Kitty, have you thought of a good reason why we can't be friends yet?" He hoped she would eventually give in and come exploring with him.

It happened exactly a week later. "Lupo, I have been trying to work out why cats and dogs can't be friends. I have spent many hours thinking up here on the kitchen cabinet or on sofa in the ballroom and I have concluded that I can't think of a good enough reason so I will be your friend."

Lupo had been ecstatic and so their friendship began. When Kitty wasn't patrolling or playing chase with him, she slept, curled up in a tight ball within a laundry basket in George's uncle's apartment.

Lupo considered himself to be a lucky spaniel. But while he had a few friends he knew that he also had a few foes. Apart from Vulcan, there was one other animal who took a lesser shine to him – whenever he met Percy, as with Vulcan, he felt like he was being watched.

Percy the pigeon spent his time sitting proudly on top of the Palace guard's house tweeting his followers. Since the arrival of the young royal family he found that he was constantly interrupted by tourists all asking where Lupo lived.

Often, Lupo heard the pompous pigeon muttering to himself, "Police bikes hum . . . that must be someone important?" all the time watching as the royal cars and helicopters came and went. The pigeon's blue and grey neck craned to get a

glimpse inside of palace matters. Percy could only dream what it was like inside Lupo's royal palace life.

Becoming a royal dog wasn't as easy as just moving into a palace. There was a lot to learn. Fortunately, Lupo considered his teacher his friend.

Herbert, a small English brown mouse, appeared one wet afternoon in the nursery a few weeks after they had moved in.

The Prince had spotted Herbert first. The mouse was desperately trying to squeeze through the drainpipe outside the nursery window. Lupo watched as the podgy brown mouse loaded up a large collection of bags and books on to a slim white mouse. (A welcoming seventh cousin called Ernie, who had been expecting his arrival.)

Herbert took time to wipe his ears and untangle a cobweb from his tail, muttering to the white mouse (who was struggling to cope with all the bags and books), "Item one on my report must be to make sure that the network is extended to allow security mice ease of access to the nursery. Item two – remove all cobwebs and other offending materials, please.

Now where is Lupo, Ernie?"

"Err, he's right in front of you," replied Ernie, pointing into the nursery through the open window.

Herbert cleared his throat and adjusted his spectacles. standing up as tall as he could. "Good, good. Lupo, a pleasure to make your acquaintance. I am Herbert, Head of Mice Intelligence Section 5 also known as M.I.5."

George wriggled on his back, curiously checking out their visitor. He murmured, "M.I. what?"

"Mice Intelligence Section 5, George. I think he is a rather important mouse." Lupo then bounded right up to Herbert. "I am Lupo and this is Prince George," he said.

Herbert bowed in the presence of the newest member of the royal family. Lupo's way of welcoming the mouse was to give him a big ol' friendly lip-smacking lick from head to toe. Herbert almost lost his serious green cardigan in the process! It was safe to say the mouse was appalled.

George was impressed by their new friend. He eagerly manoeuvred himself to the front of the cot so he could watch the animals. Still clutching his wombat, he stuck his thumb in his mouth, wide eyed. He was waiting to see what would happen between the mouse and Lupo next.

Before Herbert could finish dressing, Lupo had him on his back and was dragging the shocked mouse out of the nursery. "Come and see the family of spiders in the pantry, Herbert. I was just telling George, they must have about a million babies! I've never seen so many of them. It's wicked. Come and check it out!"

"LUPO! I am not here to play. I am here to teach you." Herbert only just managed to wriggle free as they arrived at the nest of young spiders.

By now, Herbert had concluded that the situation was worse than he had imagined. The cocker spaniel needed lessons in *everything* from royal history, English, Latin and combat training to geography and mathematics. Teaching him these would be easy – just as it was with any of the Queen's dogs. Apart from Vulcan, that was. Privately, Herbert suspected the Queen's special dorgi was the runt of his litter. But to Herbert the big difference between Lupo and the corgis was that they were already royalty. They had manners and knew how to behave.

He started by trying to teach Lupo some manners.

Rolling up his sleeves, he looked at his tiny watch and said, "The entire animal kingdom is looking forward to seeing what kind of a royal dog you will become. There's no time to waste!"

When Herbert saw Lupo with the spiders, he understood there was something special about Lupo. The spiders seemed to flock around the spaniel. He played with the young babies and talked to their overjoyed parents.

This royal dog *was* special. Animals liked him. Prince George liked him, too. Lupo was the friendliest royal dog Herbert had ever met.

Their friendship bloomed quickly. Lupo loved listening to Herbert tell him about the history of the nation and its hidden treasures whilst George napped. Lupo's hard work was paying off. Pretty soon he had learnt some royal manners and a great deal about the world around him.

Then, one day, as they neared the end of yet another lesson, Herbert became more serious.

"Now with all the history within the palaces there are of course a few oddities," he warned mysteriously. "I won't go into all of them just yet – most you will discover for yourself in your own time. For now you must focus on trying to be a good royal dog. Never forget your job is to serve your family. Take care of Prince George and guard the palace. Most of all, don't forget that being royalty means that you could end up having all sorts of grand experiences."

As it turned out, Lupo didn't have to wait long for his first royal adventure.

3
The Queen's Bacon

Not too far from Kensington Palace, Her Majesty the Queen was stretching in her peach nightgown and curlers.

Vulcan's ears pricked up as he heard the breakfast tray coming up the stairs. Bacon, *yes*! he caught a faint whiff of the very best Gloucestershire bacon. Vulcan's stomach grumbled unhappily from his dog bed. His beady eyes looked around the royal bedroom at the corgis. He was meant to be her special one.

Watching Monty sitting on a cushion staring at the Queen made him lurch with revulsion. He detested that corgi. Next, his gaze came to rest on Holly. She yawned lazily as she lay next to Her Majesty's comfortable and practical pink slippers.

Willow was chasing something in her sleep.

Finally he took in the splendour that was Candy. He loved her so deeply and yet she continually failed to notice him. Candy only had eyes for the baby George's uncle. Vulcan may as well have not existed. She stood, perfectly manicured and groomed, waiting by the door for the royal breakfast's arrival.

Thankfully, being the eldest dog, he didn't bother spending anytime with Her Majesty's "other" dogs. He preferred to keep himself to himself. He kept saying under his bad breath, "One day they all will be gone and it will be just ME – as it should be."

Vulcan, the loner, looked on from his bed behind the heavy chintzy palace curtains, plotting. Outside, he could hear the birds in the garden. Somewhere in the distance a car alarm sounded, and then a police van.

Buckingham Palace was his home and where business was conducted, but he found London noisy and longed to get back to Balmoral. The old Scottish castle – which was one of the Queen's country residences – was so quiet you could hear the royal mice gossiping in the corridors at night. No one seemed to notice how much he missed his heather.

Rolling on the moors was one of Vulcan's pleasures in life; quietly sniffing the roses in the main garden was the other. But in London the roses were permanently covered in manure from the royal stables and if by chance he should get a moment to enjoy them, he found their smell tainted by the traffic whirling around Hyde Park Corner.

Now Vulcan watched as the Queen zipped up her light blue dressing gown and picked up the receiver of the peach telephone by the bed. He listened as she repeated the day's schedule to her private secretary.

Vulcan could hear the Queen talking about Kensington Palace. She asked after her great grandson. Then she laughed as the private secretary said something about Lupo. There was an article about him in today's newspaper. Vulcan's fur bristled unpleasantly.

The Queen replaced the receiver and asked for a second pot of English breakfast tea. Today was a two-pot day. Her Majesty seemed tired as she yawned loudly.

Tommy the footman returned with a refreshed pot and covered it with a knitted tea cozy bearing the royal standard.

The Queen sipped her tea from a fine Coronation china cup. Vulcan watched and waited till she put the cup down. The dogs, knowing her routine, jostled for position, all trying to get her attention. Vulcan had seen enough. He took himself off to the bedroom door on his stout little legs and sat looking back at the royal dogs, all sitting and begging for the Queen's scraps.

Tommy opened the door to collect today's newspaper, sent up from the private secretary for Her Majesty's amusement. The article on Lupo was on the front page.

Vulcan sneered as the kindly footman gave it to the Queen. The door remained ajar. He took his opportunity to get out.

The Queen broke her bacon into small pieces. Today all the dogs got a bit of the Queen's bacon – everyone except for Vulcan.

Her Majesty was downstairs in her weekly meeting with the Prime Minister. Most of the previous Prime Ministers had not been comfortable with the Queen's dogs being present. Vulcan suspected they were "afraid of dogs". The current Prime Minster was an

exception. He loved dogs, or so he claimed. Whilst the corgis made a fuss of him, leaving white hairs all over his blue suit and paw marks on his lap, Vulcan had crept back upstairs to the royal bedchamber.

The maids were busy vacuuming and cleaning. He hid behind the curtains, waiting for them to leave him in peace. He had work to do. The time had come to act.

As the Hoover buzzed its way out into the main corridor, he watched the Head Housekeeper click her biro and tick her clipboard. The Queen's chamber was his at last.

Envy clouded his judgement and consumed his thoughts. "There has to be a way of turning the tide back in my favour. I need to get rid of Lupo, then they will all see that I am the royal dog." Vulcan's heart was racing. Terror and anger gripped his mind. He whispered out loud. "The answer is simple: destroy Lupo and I will be the hero. I need a distraction – something big, terrifying and brilliant that I can control."

Jumping on to the Queen's bed, he ran over to

her private diary, which was sitting on her bedside table. Snatching it with his teeth, he dragged it to the middle of the bed and flicked it open.

The diary was filled with the day's events, worries for the nation and notes on the family. The diary was knowledge and this meant power. Fifty years of the nation's secrets were buried in her handwriting. He needed only one, something that had the power to change everything.

"President this and Prime Minister that . . . blah, blah, blah," he whispered to himself, frustration kicking in. He flicked the priceless pages back and forward, reading Her Majesty's innermost fears and thoughts. He was about to tear the book to pieces "Nothing! NOTHING!" then – there it was.

He stopped. Slowly, he took in every word, again and again. Wincing, he followed the blue ink on the white page.

St George's Day, 23 April.

I am worried about the continued protection of the 'Windsor Secret'.

New Member of the Order of Ascalon was overheard openly discussing its security around the Prime Minister.

What if the most dangerous creature known to man ever did get out?

I fear for my people's safety. I wish there was a way to destroy it for once and for all . . .

As he slammed the diary closed, an evil grin crept across Vulcan's face. This was exactly what he had been looking for. He had his answer.

4
The Windsor Secret

Vulcan knew that the truth about the Windsor Secret had to be locked within the Queen's private safe. Located in her bathroom at Buckingham Palace (behind a watercolour of the south-east corner of Windsor Castle, by Paul Sandby, *c.* 1765) the safe contained all sorts of important things. But it was a series of documents and private letters that Vulcan was most interested in reading.

Vulcan was able to get into the safe as everyone slept. Since he followed the Queen at all times he knew the entry code. The safe opened and from it he pulled a volume of letters written to Edward the Confessor and some papers signed by William the Conqueror. The papers painted a bleak picture of England. The Lord Chancellor had written that the young nation was broke thanks to the building of a fort at Windsor and a fleet of large ships. *"A vessel large enough to bring a dragon from the farthest corner of England,"* the worried treasurer had written.

Vulcan kept reading, his excitement building.

There was a note on the back of the paper addressed to a young villager called George recording the payment of gold and the promise of a sainthood. Vulcan knew that it was highly unusual for a King to grant a sainthood.

"For what? Why would little old George get a sainthood?" he said, aloud. Reading on, he suddenly froze. *"Capture of the Dragon."* The words jumped out at him. "St George and the dragon!"

Vulcan's whiskers twitched. He knew the story well. Finally, he understood. *"George and the dragon . . . the legend of St George . . . the finest fable in England . . . not a fable after all . . ."* Then, rereading the letters and notes, he did a double-take. His eyes moved like the shutter of a camera over the word *"Capture."*

George had captured the dragon, and not slain it. George was made a saint not for saving England but for capturing a dragon and bringing it to the small original Anglo-Saxon fort at Windsor – *ALIVE*.

The last of the papers was in St George's rough farm-boy words. It spoke in Old English of a ring he had made that was needed to assert authority over the dragon – "*the bearer of which controls the beast. My sword is its only fear. For the beast knows that it is the only sword that has a blade sharp enough to pierce its black scaly skin!*"

Vulcan feverishly turned the pages, reading and re-reading, as the true story of St George and the dragon was revealed.

King William was so concerned about an enemy invasion and the troublesome Welsh, he decided to keep the dragon as a secret weapon. George had lured the dragon on to a ship and then sailed it into a cave within Windsor Castle. William's dragon was now safely hidden away.

Vulcan knew that the noble Order of Ascalon was formed on the deathbed of King William. History claimed that as the King lay dying, he had summoned his noble and loyal Knights of the Realm.

Twenty-four of the bravest Knights stood in a circle around the King as he told them that they had to hide the sword and ring and at all costs. "*You must never let anyone find my dragon,"* said the dying King.

The Knights of the Realm obeyed their King and took the sword and the ring to the very last place anyone would look, throwing them both into the middle of a deep dark pond.

Vulcan recalled his royal history lessons with Herbert. They had discussed many ancient animal legends. St George and the dragon was a popular story. Piecing together this human story and the more popular animal story he was able to work out exactly where this pond was located. His entire coat tingled. An awful vicious plan crystallized in his mind. He knew exactly how to find the sword and destroy Lupo.

Vulcan read more, discovering that the new King, Edward, had tortured the Knights, trying to discover where the secret ring and sword had been hidden. None of the Knights would tell him.

Years of searching led to nothing. Edward gave up, writing that *"the last place to look is the hidden pond."* But Vulcan knew that the pond had never been searched because on the last page was a desperate note from the Lord Chancellor complaining, *"No money – England's gold and wealth disappeared with that dragon.*" And then finally, "*Abandon this folly!*"

Edward had given up. St George and the dragon became a myth. Lost in time.

"A sleeping dragon, controlled by whoever wields the Ascalon sword and wears the St George's ring . . . and it sleeps on a bed of English gold." Vulcan laughed, a dangerous glimmer showing in his eyes. He licked his lips – he knew where they were. "This was better than I could have ever hoped! Ha! NO one will question me again! I will have all the power." Vulcan excitedly held his breath. "I will have this dragon. I will control this country. I will destroy anyone who gets in my way. And best of all . . . I will destroy Lupo in the process."

5
The Meeting of Minds

Vulcan knew he was going to need help if he was going to get the ring and the sword out of the hidden pond. The help came when he was least expecting it.

At night time, a few days later, he caught a male buck rat foraging for food in the larder at Buckingham Palace. It was a vicious, nasty, dirty-looking thing. It snarled and he only just managed to back the dark creature into a corner. Under the glare of an exposed bulb he threatened to punish it for its crime.

"I'm not bowing to the likes of you, *dog*," said the rodent.

"Oh yes you will, or I will destroy you. I could tear you limb from limb. You will obey me."

"You haven't got the chops . . . you're just a fussy,

spoilt dog!" the rat spat back.

Vulcan stood his ground and bared his teeth. Slowly, he edged his way closer to the rat. They were nose to nose. "BOW or DIE . . . your choice."

The rat was unable to run. Vulcan grabbed it with a stubby but powerful paw.

"What do you want me to bow for – haven't you got enough slaves, here in this palace of yours?" The rat could feel the paw tightening around his neck.

"You're right. I have servants. I get everything I need. Do you, RAT? Do *you* have everything you want? Everything your heart desires?"

Vulcan had the rat exactly where he wanted him. The rat looked confused and unsure for the first time. "What's it to you?" it dared ask.

"You see, my rodent friend, I can help you. I have the means to give you anything you want. How about this? Some cake perhaps? Strawberries and cream? Chocolate biscuits?"

The rat was curious. Vulcan began throwing food on to the floor. The rat bent down to grab at it, too delicious not to take.

"Take more, take it all – there is plenty more where it came from. If you serve me I will give you everything you will ever want," said Vulcan. "But if you choose not to help me I will destroy you right now."

The rat looked into Vulcan's eyes and knew the dog was completely serious. It lowered itself further to the ground. Its cheeks were still bulging with cake and biscuits. "I serve another. I already have a master . . ." it stammered.

Vulcan struck the rat's face with his paw. "You think there could be a higher command than me?"

The rat knew his luck was up. He would have to serve two masters. He needed the food. His wife, Mrs Claw, was due to give birth again any day now and with his ever-increasing family he couldn't afford to not have access to the royal larder. "Begging your pardon, no, sir, forgive my mistake."

"Name?"

"Claw, sir, Claw."

Vulcan wanted to see just how desperate the rat was. He followed it down to the City of Creatures beneath Buckingham Palace where it said it lived. They walked into the darkest part of the city. Urban foxes looked at them suspiciously. Rats spied on them.

The tunnels were in a terrible state. The brickwork had crumbled, and tree roots had taken hold of the interior. One of the first royal tunnels to have been abandoned, it hadn't been used since the last execution at the Tower of London.

He was amused to see how many animals nested here. There were houses and even a few animal shops and what appeared to be a rat-infested hotel open along the route.

Behind The Dog and Duck Tavern – a pub run by a dog and a duck – was a betting shop. Crowds of desperate-looking rats, mice and small birds barely noticed the dog as they gambled their precious food on a rodent race.

They arrived at a small slum dwelling, constructed mainly of bits of broken sewer pipe and used tin-can lids. Playing cards tacked together with used thread passed for a roof, and inside, in a nest lined with scraps of soiled linen, slept four scrawny young rats, their ribcages visible as they breathed. It was the first case of squalor the royal dorgi had seen. Allergic to the poor, he sneezed, dislodging a playing-card tile from the roof.

"Mrs Claw, I've got bread and cheese and a royal

guest. This is His Highness, Vulcan. This is our humble home, sir," the rat announced.

"But, I thought that Edgar was . . ." said Mrs Claw quietly to her husband.

"Mrs Claw, this is my Master, His Highness, Vulcan," said Claw.

"Oh I see . . . I just thought . . ." Hastily she tried to tidy away piles of dirty rags and scraps of paper she was collecting for the young rats' new homes.

"Hmm . . ." Vulcan was unimpressed with Mrs Claw and her squalid home. Trying hard not to breathe the fetid air he looked down his short nose at them. "This is suitable accommodation – for a rat – is it?"

"Yes, sir, it really is very useful having an underground network so close. I'll never be late for work, sir," Claw interjected.

From a small pouch tied to his collar, Vulcan took out a biscuit and tossed it to the sleeping rats. The Claws fell before him in gratitude, but, fearing he'd be touched, the dog held up his paw to stop them. "Enough!" he commanded. "Just remember this, Claw: serve me well and you and your family will be fed. Fail me, and . . . well, let's not frighten the babies by talking of the consequences."

The rat put his forefeet together and bowed, then, tugging his forelock, eyed up the pouch around the dog's neck and asked, "How can I serve you, Master?"

Mrs Claw uttered a second time, "But I thought Edgar . . ." She was silenced again by a look of annoyance and anger from her ratty husband.

Vulcan made himself comfortable. "Firstly, I want the Ascalon Sword and the Ring of St George – get them for me."

"From where?" queried the rat.

Vulcan answered in a whisper. "They are under guard. In the waters beneath the Imperial Swans."

"The Serpentine Lake?" Claw replied. The Serpentine Lake was the most secure animal location. No animal dared to interfere with the Imperial Swans.

"Yes, that's right – once nothing more than a murky pond more commonly referred to as the hidden pond."

"You're telling me the sword and the ring are in the water?"

"Yes, I suspect they have been there for a very long time. You will need to recover them."

"That's always been the home of the Imperial Swans. Those birds are big – I don't think they would like me in their water, disturbing the peace and such; not to be messed with. Protected birds and all that." Claw was growing nervous. He had never been asked to do something so tricky. As a buck rat he could swim well. It was dealing with the swans that guarded the Serpentine Lake that bothered him.

Mrs Claw felt Vulcan's creepy paws around her shoulders. He was squeezing her, threatening her as he spoke to Claw. "I have been watching the swans. There is one that guards the water at night. His name is Cyrus. Do what you must to overpower him."

"I'm not getting caught and imprisoned for harming one of those birds. I have a family. You're asking too much."

"It's simple, Claw, do as I say or . . ." He squeezed Mrs Claw more tightly and looked at the sleeping rats. "Never see your family again."

"You need to tell me why! Why do you want the ring and the sword? And why do you want to harm Cyrus? What is this all about?"

Vulcan said, "Lupo." His small dark eyes seemed

to turn darker at the mention of the royal dog's name. Claw felt the small home grow colder.

"The Duke and Duchess's dog? I don't understand."

"He will be blamed for the bird. He will suffer the wrath of the animal kingdom. The royal family will disown him for his treachery. The sword and the ring are . . . trinkets . . . priceless trinkets, that's all." Vulcan quivered with excitement.

The full horror of his plan was now clear to the Claws. "How am I meant to do that?" Claw stared back at Vulcan, whose eyes were now concentrated on Mrs Claw's three babies, unaware of what was happening, asleep in their rags.

"Find a way, Claw. You must have friends down here – friends who need food and royal protection?"

"The squirrels really hate the dogs – I'm pretty sure I could get one of them to help me – but it will cost . . . a lot . . . they don't come cheap, Your Highness."

"Make it happen, Claw. Get a squirrel to help you and I will reward you both. Above all, Lupo must be there when it happens. Only by harming an Imperial Swan will the family question his suitability as a royal dog. I want him out of the palace . . . gone . . . for good. Make sure it is done. No mistakes."

Vulcan opened the pouch and removed what remained of a bacon sandwich. Prince George's uncle had been eating it on a flying visit to Buckingham Palace that morning. Mrs Claw descended on the meal and, within seconds, was begging her royal visitor for more.

"Oh there is plenty more for you, just make sure your husband does exactly what I want!"

"Yes, understood, Your Royal-ness!" she replied humbly.

6
The Ascalon Sword

The lake was dark and motionless. A full moon cast eerie shadows in between the branches of Kensington Gardens' old and withered trees. The wind whispered through the frozen bushes, rasping on ragged and crumpled leaves. Autumn was over now. Winter was back and it was shaking its fist – at every fish, mammal and bird.

In a corner of the park strangely neglected by visitors, wardens and gardeners, Cyrus the Imperial Swan shifted uncomfortably on the edge of the lake. He removed his King James Bible from his knapsack and propped it against a rock. Wearily, he looked around. Nothing stirred. The wind had subsided, and the park now seemed almost unnaturally calm, stilled by the spreading frost. There would barely be a

59

sound, but for his sighs.

He had not wanted to leave for work on this cold night. Cyrus was finding his role as the lake's guardian very lonely. Night after night he sat guarding in the dark. Before he had left the nest, he had shuffled close to his wife, Marie Louise, seeking comfort. She had reminded him of his duty to his family. "You must go tonight. It is your job. Cygnets will be born any day now and they need a father that can protect his home."

Now on the bank, he fought sleep. He lit his candle and took out his glasses, but his eyes were too tired to read. Sometime after ten o'clock, he fell into a deep sleep. His glasses fell down the side of his beak. He did not hear the buck rat break the icy surface of the lake.

It was not Claw's first time in the cold water. For several nights he had worked undisturbed as the swan slept on its rock. He'd clawed through the tangled mess of overgrown watery weeds and, each time, swum a little further and a little deeper. His challenge, which had seemed impossible, was now nearing completion. He could sense triumph. He could smell it; he could almost *taste* the treats he was destined to receive. This night, he knew he would find what he was looking for. He took a large gulp of air through his whiskered nose and then one through his fanged mouth – and dived hard and fast to the depths.

It was dark down on the bottom. Slippery frogspawn and rotting branches lay on top of fish skeletons and stones. The rat had to work hard. Churning up the sandy clay bottom, he dug around, seeking the objects Vulcan desired.

The water above him rippled and Cyrus awoke. The swan saw him rear to the surface for air.

Claw's slimy hairless grey tail twitched as the huge white bird entered the water. Claw turned downwards and pushed himself deeper still. Rummaging around, forcing over a rock, he found a fish laying strings of eggs. The fish tried to swat him away but he bit her as he broke through her newly laid eggs.

Flicking his tail furiously, the rat propelled his large, strong body through the water. He moved faster and faster – and, within minutes, found the oak box. "At last!" he thought.

Pulling the box from the deep, he forced it open.

Inside, lay the Ascalon Sword. Delicately engraved, it had remained buried for centuries – until this night, this terrible, unnatural night.

The rat lifted it from its red velvet bed inside the box and, with all his might, swung it through the water.

At the top, Cyrus searched in vain for the intruder. Swimming back to his post and seeing the female fish die, he reacted quickly, unfurling his wings and flapping as hard as possible. As he did so, the rat broke the surface with the sword in his cold wet paw.

Cyrus felt the icy cold blade slice through his wing and as it did, the St George's Ring that had been passed down from his forefathers, fell on to the rock beside the water's edge.

Claw moved quickly now. The bird was alive, but he had harmed it badly. The mission was done. He felt no remorse, all he wanted to do was get out of the water and get home to Mrs Claw. Vulcan would be pleased with his work.

Cyrus made no noise as he tried to pull himself out of the water.

Grabbing the ring, Claw slipped it around his neck and, dragging the sword, struggled toward the

same storm drain on the North bank he had used nightly to get in and out of the lake.

Without looking back, he fled down the tunnel, his reward tonight being that his family would eat like royalty.

Cyrus's proud neck flopped forward, and his orange and black beak crashed like a glass into the icy waters. He struggled back to the bank, every movement leading to loss of blood. He knew what he had to do. Feathers from his mutilated wing still floated at the water's edge. He plucked one free with his beak and began to draw something into the muddy bank. It was a noble gesture of an Imperial Swan. His blood flowed out of his wounds and into the drawing. He worked until dawn's early light, growing fainter with every second that passed. When he was finished, he lay waiting for help.

7

Lupo's Discovery

Next morning, the Duchess was distracted by a telephone call and walked to the little blue sofa at the end of the nursery. Covering the mouthpiece, she whispered to Nanny that it was the Queen's Private Secretary and could she dress Prince George? Nanny nodded and disappeared to fetch George's clothes for the day, leaving him bouncing happily in his walker.

The Duchess scribbled notes whilst on the phone. Her diamond and sapphire ring caught a ray of winter sun and glinted brightly, filling the nursery with twinkling lights. Prince George gurgled contentedly at the lights now darting all over the ceiling.

Lupo jumped on to the chair besides the changing table, sniffing: "Any minute, George, and we will be

65

out there. I can't wait. How many squirrels today, huh? I bet I can chase at least three."

George laughed and shrilled, "Three!"

Nanny returned, shooing Lupo off the chair. "Get down, Lupo! Royal cocker spaniels do not jump up on baby's chair! Down, you black beast!"

Nanny wagged her finger at the royal dog. She did not approve of dogs (or cats for that matter) in the nursery, and she certainly didn't want anyone over-exciting the Prince – or disturbing the Duchess's call with Buckingham Palace.

Meanwhile, standing in the corridor, Kitty watched events unfold gleefully, giggling behind her soft tabby paw. There was nothing she liked better than seeing Nanny get cross with Lupo – from a safe and comfortable distance, of course.

Lupo growled playfully at Nanny, his black silky head with its happy shiny eyes cocked to one side.

"Oh, don't give me those I'm-too-cute-to-be-in-trouble eyes, young pup," Nanny commanded. "Just because everyone else gives you what you want, it doesn't mean I'm going to let you disturb the heir to the throne from having a proper walk! Now be gone with you, you furry monster!"

Lupo crawled under the cot. Underneath, he rolled on a clean cream carpet. Stretching his paws, he scratched the bottom of the cot.

Above him, George continued to mutter – something about wanting another egg, and perhaps a biscuit. Lupo stopped playing when he noticed the snow on the branches of an old English oak outside the nursery window.

"SNOW, GEORGE, SNOW!" he exclaimed in a series of excited barks.

George let out the biggest yell ever – he didn't know what snow was.

Grooling, growling, and adding a few long yawns, Lupo tried to explain what snow was to the little prince. "It's white and soft and incredibly fluffy and cold all at the same time! Oh George, this is the best thing about winter. We have to get out there . . . now!"

George and Lupo both erupted into pure excitement. Nanny couldn't take all the noise. The Duchess, off her call, walked back to the cot. Reaching down, she kissed her son's head. Narrowly, she missed treading on Lupo as he twisted around and around her navy-blue heels in happiness.

"Your Royal Highness, I think it is time for Prince

George's walk. Shall I take Lupo?"

"Time for a walk, everyone?" The Duchess clapped merrily, causing the noise level to erupt to new highs. "Nanny, I think you have your answer! Have fun everyone and enjoy the snow!"

Bolting down the corridor, Lupo almost knocked a chambermaid over. He found his collar and leash on a little green wooden bench by the back door. Racing back to the nursery with everything in his mouth, he came to a skidding halt by the kitchen, colliding with Kitty.

The cat staggered to her feet and hissed at him. "Stop racing round, hound. You're making me dizzy. What's the fuss about anyhow? That park's full of all sorts of nasty dirty animals . . . Then again, you'd fit in, I suppose!"

Lupo narrowed his furry brows and tried to look serious, but his enthusiasm ruined the effect. "It's snowing, Kitty! Why don't you come with us? Come and play with me!" He begged her, "It really is totally awesome out there. Come on! Let's chase some squirrels together!"

Kitty raised her eyebrow in return and promptly replied, "Calm down, and stop panting in my face!

Whoever heard of a cat chasing a squirrel? I don't think so. Be gone, you pampered pup!"

She sashayed up the corridor in the direction of George's uncle's apartment.

Three tourists were discussing who should have the last blue hire bike in the rack at the top of Albert Gate. Lupo wasn't interested in what they were saying as he trotted past. He was busy thinking how pretty the park looked today. The snow had fallen and it lay all around but the sun was shining. Kensington's park had become a magical, snowy playground.

The park was full to bursting with people running and playing in the soft snow. Dogs ran in between the trees whilst their owners hunkered in their coats and scarves on old green iron benches. Everywhere he looked, Lupo could see people. Young children screaming and giggling, old people laughing and chatting. Bikes, scooters, roller-skates were all around. It was all very exciting. Sniffing the air he could smell wet, snowy grass, sandwiches, hot chocolate and squirrels.

Much to Nanny's distress, Lupo began pulling

hard on his lead. Giving up trying to control the baby buggy and the dog, she freed him and that was it. The park was his.

Lupo took off like lighting in the direction of the palace's pretty Rose Garden pond.

With a clatter of hooves and a very loud *neigh*, one of the Queen's horses swerved, narrowly missing the speeding pup. "Slow down, Lupo!" called out the horse.

Lupo ran through the gates marked "NO DOGS" and all the way to the pond. He was dying to see all the animals. He peered down at the water's edge and gave a lopsided smile at his own reflection. Then he took a giant leap and landed SPLASH! in the icy cold water.

Below, a large carp stared up at Lupo's big feet. The fish disliked the fact that there was a dog evidently enjoying himself, swimming round and round in circles above him. "Whatever next," he bubbled to himself.

Lupo lapped up the water and aimed for some ducks – perhaps they would like to play today. "Hi!" shouted Lupo at the ducks.

But the ducks were also unhappy about being

disturbed – a group of children had thrown bread crumbs into the water. The food had been sitting on top of the soft green pond algae for hours, giving them every opportunity to get it all before the fish got it. Unfortunately Lupo had swum right through it and now the fish were enjoying what was meant to be the ducklings' lunch. The noisy dog had no place in the Rose Garden pond so they promptly got out and waddled off in the direction of the public pond in the middle of the park.

Lupo was confused: normally everyone was happy to see him and he couldn't understand why the ducks had ignored him and gone away.

He struggled to get out of the pond. The animals all round were all laughing as he heaved his wet body, covered in tangled reeds, out of the water.

Two beautiful green parrots were resting on a branch nearby. They looked at Lupo and turned to each other, their pretty beaks chattering quickly, "I'm telling you, Paulo, that dog should not be in the pond. What on earth does he think he's doing there?"

"Chica, my love, you can squawk! We should be in the rainforest, not the middle of Kensington Gardens, London!"

Paulo looked around him, admiring the snow that had gathered on the branches of the trees. "I know, but Lupo *gets* it – there is something very special here in Kensington. I'm glad we are going to be here for a while."

Lupo shook off the water and began to run towards the Princess Diana Playground, dragging long strands of bright green pond weed with him. He loved the feeling of the playground sand between his paws. He ran up the pirate ship gangway and through the porthole window, joyfully grabbing the ropes of the mast!

"Ha ha," he cried. "A pirate's life for me!" and then he jumped out and rang the bell on the end of the ship before setting off again. Little did he realize he had managed to cover the entire ship in green pond weed! Toddlers were watching and they ran to grab the slimy, cold strings.

Nanny was calling for Lupo. As he ran back to her, he barked, excited to have spotted his first squirrel. There was something odd about this creature though. Normally, the squirrels would see him and run as fast as their tiny paws could carry them to the safety of the nearest tree. But this squirrel was running directly at him. Never in all the months he had been playing in the park had a squirrel actively tried to play with him.

"Hi there! I'm Lupo – what's your—" he began, but stopped in his tracks. The squirrel seemed to be summoning him: encouraging him to follow it. At no point did it try to dash up a tree or scamper on to a bench, it was acting highly irregularly.

"What's your name?" he woofed, thoroughly enjoying this new game.

The squirrel didn't answer him. Lupo was inches from its flicking grey tail. It jumped high in the sky, using Nanny's ample form as a shield, jumping clean over the baby carriage and scurrying towards a row of bushes.

George squirmed in his pram. "I saw it! I saw it jumping!"

Lupo was determined to chase the squirrel for as long as he carried its scent. He found it waiting for him at the corner of a long pathway leading to the Albert Memorial. The chase was back on. A gardener dressed in green overalls shook his broom as they both raced through the finely manicured grounds.

The squirrel dived into a tangled blackberry bush.

Lupo fought his way through, his long tail wagging frantically. He was in no doubt – victory was almost his, if he could just get beyond the overgrown, snow-covered bush.

The squirrel came to a stop and stood on the spot. It watched as Lupo squeezed his way in. The squirrel stood with her small paws on her hips, next to an old, overgrown pond.

"Thanks to you, dumb dog, I won't have to work this winter – I'll be feasting on nuts and berries. HA!" The squirrel laughed. "Now you can feel what it's like to be hunted!" It stood back to reveal the most terrifying sight – Cyrus, but the beautiful swan's eyes were closed and he was barely breathing. Snowflakes settled on his body.

Lupo didn't know what to do first. He wasn't looking or listening to the squirrel any more. Instead, he was concentrating on the pile of white feathers littered all over the lake's surface and along the water's edge. There wasn't time to dwell. He leaped into action, desperate to help the poorly swan. "HELP!" he barked, turning to the squirrel, but it was gone. The joyful morning turned sour in his mouth.

Racing over to the swan it was clear to Lupo that

Cyrus had been attacked by something very heavy and sharp. "Wake up, please wake up." The swan's eyes opened briefly: it spoke. "Protect the secret," were Cyrus's last words before he fell into a deep sleep.

"Protect the secret? No, wake up, wake up. I can get help." Lupo looked around. Then he saw the Shield of St George, sketched into the mud. The swan had drawn it with his uninjured wing together with the letter "S". Lupo needed to move the bird to see what the word said so gently, he took the bird's neck in his mouth and began to pull it out of the lake's edge and towards a tree.

At that same moment the bushes parted and staring at him was a horrified park warden. High in the trees above, a squadron of Magpie Police Birds appeared. The royal warden spoke. "LET GO OF THE BIRD, LUPO!"

Cowering under the tree, feeling the bird's heartbeat slowing down, he then heard one of the magpies squawk, "LUPO, STEP AWAY FROM CYRUS!"

There was nothing to be done. Lupo was relieved that he was not alone and that someone would help the poor swan. But he also knew that they all thought he had harmed the bird. So many angry eyes looked at him, accusing him of a crime he had not committed.

"*Woof, woof, grrh!*" he cried. "Please help him. I think he is dying!"

But the warden didn't understand Lupo's language and was taken aback by the barking. He sprung forward, grabbing Lupo's body, pulling him away from the swan.

Just as he was being carried out of the bushes, Lupo looked down and saw the words "Slay the dragon" beneath the sleeping swan.

The park warden held on to him tightly – there was nowhere to run. Nanny was crying, clutching Prince George, who didn't understand what was happening. All she kept saying was, "Lupo would never attack a swan – he is just not like that, please don't hurt him."

The park warden looked at Lupo and then spoke, "In all my years with the Royal Parks I have never seen a dog go for a swan. I'm sorry, Nanny, I think this dog is very dangerous. We had better get him back to the Duke and Duchess and let them decide his fate."

"Oh my, oh dear," replied Nanny, who was cradling Prince George.

Lupo felt weak and scared. The nightmare from last night was real. The only thing missing was the dragon and the evil bark. He sniffed the air, trying to smell grass, anything that might comfort him, but all he could smell was blood – the swan's blood – which was all over his paws.

The Duke and Duchess sat in the living room. Lupo sat between them, wrapped in a wet towel. The Duchess placed her long fingers on his black head.

"Your Highness, I would suggest that he be put down," said the warden. "There's no knowing what he is capable of. Far be it for me to tell you, but I know I wouldn't dream of having a young baby around such a dangerous dog."

The Duke nodded, and stood up. He thanked the warden for his troubles and showed him out. The Duchess had begun to cry. When the Duke returned they agreed that it was probably for the best that Lupo be locked in the kitchen until they could decide what to do with him.

George's tears flowed. Nanny carried him to the nursery. "*Dodo!*" he said "*Dodo!*" he cried. There was nothing Lupo could do.

Sniffing, he tried to say something to calm his friend. "It was the dragon. I'm going to find it. I'll be back soon. It's all OK."

That did it. George was happy again at the thought of Lupo going off on an adventure. He blew a dribble-bubble which meant, "Lucky you!" Then he roared, as best a baby can, his chubby hands grabbing the air like sharp claws.

Lupo hung his head low as George disappeared. Saddened and confused, he took himself off to the kitchen. As the door shut, he jumped into his unused bed. It was cold and dark. He made no sound. Instead, he sat thinking.

Cyrus had not revealed who his attacker had been. He had said only "Protect the secret" and had written, "Slay the dragon" beneath the shield of St George. They had to be clues.

Lupo lay down, and began to work out what had happened. First, he remembered the way the squirrel had looked at him – it was odd. That squirrel had definitely been leading him to the Swan. Lupo began to wonder if he had been set up. He recalled what the strange squirrel had said. *"Thanks to you, dumb dog, I won't have to work this winter – I'll be feasting on nuts and berries."* Then she had said something that now convinced him he'd been set up. *"Now you can feel what its like to be hunted."*

"A trap! That's exactly what that was! I was a fool, I walked straight into it," he said aloud in the dark.

"Yes, you did," came a voice out of the darkness.

Lupo heard Kitty's soft voice meowing. She then flicked the kitchen light on with her tabby tail and jumped down to the side of his bed.

"Kitty, I was set up. That squirrel wanted me to find the swan."

Kitty stretched. She had been on the prowl when she had heard about the swan. She was worried about Lupo. He was her friend. She had to help him.

"What you need to work out is who and why someone would trap you like that. Do you have anyone who would want to hurt you, Lupo? Anyone who would want you out of the palace?"

Lupo thought hard. He was convinced that there

80

was no one who wanted to harm him. "No." Then his thoughts turned to Vulcan. The only animal that might want him gone. Vulcan was someone who didn't think he fitted in. "Hang on – it could be . . . VULCAN."

"Are you sure?"

"Yes – when I first met him he seemed aggravated by me. Holly said it was something to do with me being a cocker spaniel and not being of royal blood. Silly stuff, really. At the time I didn't take it seriously. I mean, who would?"

"Lupo, the nation has taken you to its heart. The people love you. You may not know this but they think of you as one of them. No royal dog has ever been given so much attention."

"Are you saying that Vulcan is jealous? That can't be – that's crazy."

Kitty knew it sounded crazy – but she also knew it was true. "I doubt many people even know his name."

Lupo wasn't convinced. "Something strange is going on. Cyrus is the key to all of this. Vulcan isn't as stupid as we'd like to think. He has a plan and hurting Cyrus was part of it. There is more to it than getting rid of me. Can you help me, Kitty? I need to get out of here."

"Getting you out of here is easy, but if you are thinking of going to the swan – well that might be hard. Cyrus was taken to the RSPCA Hospital somewhere in Putney. It's going to be touch and go if he makes it. It was a pretty bad attack. He lost a lot of blood."

"He told me to 'Protect the secret'," said Lupo. "I can't understand why he would say that or what he meant. It's important I find out why."

"The swan spoke to you? Didn't he tell you who hurt him?" Kitty enquired.

"No, he didn't. If I can't get to Cyrus then I need to start with the squirrel – it has to have some answers. It was given a reward of winter food in exchange for leading me to the scene of the crime."

Kitty began cleaning herself, one long lick after the other along her brown dappled paws. "This is dirty business – it makes me feel very unclean." Pausing, she looked up. "You had better tidy this mess up fast or else . . ." She had said too much.

Lupo looked despairingly into Kitty's soft face. "What is it that you are not telling me, Kitty? What are they going to do to me if I don't find out who did this?"

Kitty was a smart cat. She saw sadness in his soft face. Reluctantly she answered him. "They're going to get rid of you. I heard the Duke talking to the warden. They said something about you being taken away."

The idea of being separated from his family was too much. Brushing it aside, he tried hard to focus on finding out who was responsible. "I need to get that squirrel."

"I hardly think this is the time for chasing squirrels, Lupo," said Kitty. "In any case, it's as bad out there in the animal world as it is in here. If you get caught by the magpies, they will lock you up. They will take you to their headquarters, where you will stay until you can be tried. That's serious stuff."

"Great! So my options are: stay here and possibly die or leave and get sent away for something I didn't do . . . Honestly, Kitty, there *are* no options. Either way I lose, but if I stay here in this bed I may never find out who did this and why."

Kitty nodded. "Well, I agree, I would want to know, too. I want to help. What can I do?"

"You said that getting out of here is easy?"

"Oh yes, I have been hoping that I would be the one to show you. I guess you are no longer a puppy any more. I don't suppose Herbert bothered to tell you about the passageways, did he?"

"No, passageways? Leading to where?"

"That's the question! Everywhere Lupo, they can take you everywhere and anywhere. Come on, I'll help you find that squirrel. Follow me, we'll have to use one of M.I.5's tunnels to access the main passageway, since all the others are buzzing with news of what happened."

"M.I.5's tunnels? Buzzing passageways?"

"Let me show you the door to the other world!" And with that, they walked off in the direction of the laundry room.

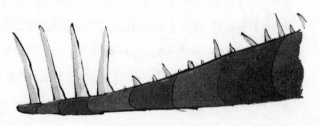

8
Mice Intelligence
Section 5

Mice Intelligence Section 5 was celebrating its hundredth year. Establishing itself had not been easy. The Magpie Police had objected to M.I.5's operations but as the network grew, animals worldwide felt safer knowing that the busy mice had their ears and eyes, fingers and tails in just about every nook and cranny, working tirelessly to keep the animal kingdom safe from the humans.

The network ran along a series of narrow routes and openings in every home, government and institution. Often thought of as the cleverest creatures in the animal world, its members had even successfully set up offices in the European palaces, all thanks to the Eurotunnel. Already, their communications were famous. If there was anything happening, M.I.5 knew all about it.

Herbert had been alone with a mountain of paperwork when he had found out about the vicious attack on Cyrus the Imperial Swan. He was used to hearing about attacks, deaths and even some strange incidents. He had files full of them but generally the animal kingdom was a pretty predictable place. Cyrus's attack was different. It was highly unusual and it was this that disturbed him. As he left his office, the latest report on the Imperial Swan's health was handed to him by a junior agent called Chloe. She seemed visibly disturbed. He took off his spectacles and asked the shaking mouse, "How bad is it?"

"It's not good. He is on the critical list, sir," she answered.

"Is he awake?"

"No, sir."

Sensing there was more, Herbert looked at the mouse, who was now looking at the floor. She was reliable and intelligent. He trusted her opinion and knew that things were particularly bad because she had a strong nose for trouble. "What's wrong?" he dared ask.

"I'm sorry, sir, something was missed from our initial report."

Herbert was concerned. Standards had to be improved. In his twenty-eight years in charge, he had never had an incomplete report. "What was missing, Chloe?"

"As you know, all the mice families in the palace like him enormously. He is helpful and considerate. We have no good reason to suspect him and let me add all the mice will agree with me. He *has* to be innocent . . ."

"Who are you talking about?" Herbert was instantly concerned.

"I am sure that when it goes to the Grand Jury they will agree. We mice are never wrong. We see and know the truth – and might I add, word is being sent out that we think he is innocent of all the charges . . ."

"Enough, Chloe – what are you talking about?"

"It was Lupo, sir. Lupo attacked the Imperial Swan. The Magpie Police reported he was seen with the victim's neck in his jaws. He's the lead suspect, sir."

Herbert grappled with a bit of paper the little

brown mouse was holding out. On it was a picture of the famous royal dog, his friend and student. He went back into his office, shut the door and closed his eyes. Vulcan was the bad royal dog, not Lupo. There had to be a mistake. Grabbing the reports from today, he stuffed them into his little briefcase and then left his office. He had to see Lupo.

Breaking into a run, he sped towards the entrance of the royal passageways. Lupo needed his help.

Access was restricted to high-ranking service agents only, but today it was filled with mice talking in small groups about Lupo.

The humans didn't bother listening to their animals, least of all trying to look for a reason as to why Cyrus had been attacked. That was his job. M.I.5 had to investigate this matter fully. As Herbert ran as fast as his small feet could carry him, past a row of mice homes with pretty pastel doors, his fifteenth cousin saw him and, waving a bag of iced buns in the air, squeaked, "My dear chap, what is the great hurry for? I have iced buns for tea!"

"No time, no time," replied Herbert, wishing that things were different. There was nothing he liked more than an iced bun and a cup of tea.

* * *

Lupo noticed that Kitty was unusually quiet. Every now and then she would stop in the middle of a corridor and look around. She was watching out for anything odd, but there was no one in sight.

She had guided him out of the kitchen via a trapdoor in the laundry room. They stood now in the middle of a small, narrow passageway, which was beneath the palace. Not far enough down to be in the sewers or the drains but low enough to only faintly hear the tourists walking on the floorboards above them. It was dark, but Kitty assured him there were better-lit passageways beyond the narrow the one they were now in.

"Be very quiet," she had told him. "I don't want to risk us being caught. We will need to tread carefully. If the magpies catch us, we will be locked up. Then we'll never find out what Vulcan is up to. So I'm not going to turn any lights on until we are clear."

Lupo nodded. He had no idea where they were. The passage was empty and unfamiliar but, as they walked along, Lupo's eyes began to adjust. He saw pictures of animals. Fine oil paintings of cats, dogs,

mice, birds all adorning the walls of the passageways. They were everywhere. Every inch taken up by the smartest pictures of hand-painted animals.

Kitty felt that they were far enough in to turn the lights on. When she did, he instantly regretted not finding the passages before. They were in a long hallway filled with the most incredible details. It was a place devoted to the hundreds of royal animals that had given service to the realm.

The largest picture was of a sleek greyhound. The sight of the proud dog filled Lupo with a kind of happiness and strength. "Is that Eos? Prince Albert's dog?" he whispered.

Kitty went on, "You could learn a lot from these animals. They stood up for what they believed in. Yes, that's Eos. He was a hero. Without him we wouldn't have these routes around the palaces. He designed them and had them extended, lit, carpeted . . ."

Lupo felt inspired. "Herbert mentioned that there were things I may discover, but he never said that there was anything like this . . . Is that a map?"

High above him he noticed that the ceilings were intricately painted with delicate arrows and pictures of palaces, parks, smart-looking official buildings and even London landmarks. Staring up, he saw that they were no longer under the palace and that they were following a thin red line which looked as though it was leading towards the middle of Hyde Park.

"This place is incredible!" he said in a soft, low voice.

The wonder of the detailing amazed him. Suddenly, the world was open to him. The thought of all the adventures and discoveries he could have using the passageways sent a shiver down his spine. He took yet more strength from the other pictures that hung all around him. The history gave him a feeling of pride. His courage swelled.

Kitty looked up at the ceiling. "It is a map. But I warn you – some of these routes haven't been used for hundreds of years. So be careful and pay attention. Stick to the Green, Red, Blue and Yellow routes only, OK? That's the only rule to follow."

Lupo was staring wide-eyed at the red line above them, trying to work it out.

Kitty said, "You see, if we stay on the red line, it will take us to Buckingham Palace. If you ask me,

Buckingham Palace is a riddle. A tricky one to navigate. The mice say that lots of them go missing there – mind the Ancient Egyptian room. Oh and careful you don't go on the Brown route – that one is a complete waste of time."

"Where does the brown one go?"

"Houses of Commons – nothing but big rats there."

As an agent, Herbert liked to blend into the background, dressed as an ordinary mouse. Instead of a uniform, he wore his hand-knitted green cardigan and a pair of horn-rimmed spectacles. The problem was, though, that over the years this *had* become his uniform, making him instantly recognizable. As he approached Kensington Palace, Percy flew down from his perch to stop him.

"Herbert, it's been a long time since we've seen you here. How can I help you?"

"I need to get into the palace. I need to see Lupo."

"Sorry, no visitors today. Lupo's locked up. Nasty business with that Imperial Swan. I suspect that's

93

the last we shall see of him."

"When did you see him, Percy?" Herbert always felt that Percy's beaky nose was sticking a little too far into Palace matters that really didn't concern him.

"This morning, 9.17 a.m. to be precise. He went off for his walk with Nanny as normal. Nothing strange about it all, except for the fact that he was clearly planning on attacking some poor creature. He was chasing round, getting into all sorts of trouble. He managed to terrorise every animal in the Rose Garden. I even witnessed him going for a squirrel – I tell you, Herbert, he's a tyrant! He was off trying to catch the poor, helpless little thing."

"Percy, do you really believe Lupo is a dangerous dog?" asked Herbert, annoyed and frustrated with the delay in letting him in.

"Oh yes, yes, yes a dangerous dog. I saw him set his sights on that very squirrel just over there. I was about to go and have my break on Victoria's head by the little fountain when I observed the attacker make his first move!" he replied, angling his pigeon feathers in the direction of an apple tree beyond the main gates. "He was off chasing it all over the park, I tell you. No way for a royal dog to behave."

Herbert ignored the pigeon's fluttering.

"If you won't listen to me, then ask the squirrel yourself. There it is! Hop on, and I'll fly you over. I wouldn't mind having a chat with it. It's often far too close to the palace for my liking – need to remind it not to cross the security line. I don't think I could handle any more trouble. No, Lupo has caused quite enough for one day."

Herbert hopped on to Percy's back, suspecting that all was not as it should be, "Hmmm, yes, I should like to hear its side of the story . . ."

When they arrived, Herbert saw that the squirrel seemed busy, rolling a very large collection of Brazil nuts under its tree. The speed at which it was moving them suggested it was in a hurry and the sheer volume of posh nuts told Herbert it was going to be in hiding beneath the tree for a long time.

A disused Victorian pump house close to the water's edge led them out into the Park. Any human really looking may have thought it odd: a shaggy black cocker spaniel and a tabby cat taking a stroll through Hyde Park. But no one noticed. Everyone was far too pre-occupied with the news vans and photographers who were gathered near the entrance to the lake.

Snapping away, the photographers seemed animated as they took pictures of the icy lake and the swans sitting on the bank huddling together. The whole world now knew about the attack, thanks to the news presenters discussing Lupo's fate.

As they made their way through the throng Lupo overheard a young pretty brunette shouting into a microphone. "We are live on the BBC. Thank you for joining me on this sad day. We'll be asking experts why a dog like Lupo would have attacked a swan and what punishment he will receive for his crime. Back to the studio for more news . . ."

Kitty pulled him away from the reporter's direction. "Ignore them. We have work to do. Look – those squirrels seem to like it round here. Maybe one of them can help point us to the squirrel you were chasing this morning." She started walking over to a pair of squirrels scurrying around the bottom of a tree.

Slowly, Lupo headed over to the twitchy creatures. Instantly, they saw him and began to move up the tree. "Please do not run away. I am only looking for information. I mean you no harm," he barked.

Twenty-five minutes later, Kitty managed to persuade a fit-looking male squirrel to come down from the middle of the tree.

"Yeah, you try anything and I will be straight back up that tree," he said wearily.

"I promise not to move. Look I'm lying down." Lupo lay as low to the ground as he could. "Please, we need help. I am looking for the squirrel that I chased this morning. I need to speak to it."

"She is no 'it', her name is Jessica. She's a crafty one. Suspect she'll be long gone by now. Got a whole year's supply of nuts from Buckingham Palace – a job well done apparently. Lucky thing, she'll be on holiday under some tree for the next six months, stuffing herself silly."

Lupo looked at Kitty, then at the squirrel. "Jessica got paid by the Palace for doing *what* exactly?"

"They say she caught you attacking the swan – she raised the alarm – saved the day. Nuts from Buckingham Palace, can you believe it? Queen's dog awarded them to her himself!"

Lupo growled. "VULCAN!"

"Yeah that's it, that's who sent them to her. Saw

the bag and everything myself. I swear those nuts came on the back of the blackest buck rat I've ever seen!"

Lupo thanked the squirrel, which darted back off up his tree. Lupo then drew a shield into the soft mud under their paws.

"What's that?" asked Kitty.

"It's the shield of St George," said Lupo. "Cyrus drew it and wrote the words, 'Slay the dragon'. He wouldn't have taken the time to do it unless it was important. I think it was a warning. I need to work out what it all means. I think it might be something to do with the fable."

Kitty began to walk back to the pump house exit. "Are you trying to tell me that this whole business has something to do with the fable of St George and the dragon? Seriously?"

"Yes, that is exactly what I am saying. I'm beginning to think that so-called 'fable' isn't a fable after all."

Kitty shrugged then shook her head. "I go to bed on a full stomach of whole milk and wake up and the world's gone crazy." A magpie circled overhead. "We have to hurry, it won't be long before word gets out that you are wandering around outside of the palace. Hurry in here . . ."

They re-entered the pump house. Kitty was right, Lupo's entire existence rested on him discovering the secret that Cyrus had almost died trying to protect.

9

Animals Gather

Herbert squeezed out of a hole between two books in the Duke's library and found both Kitty and Lupo sitting on the floor in the middle of the kitchen, deep in thought. "There you are!" he exclaimed.

Herbert adjusted his cardigan so that the little buttons were all properly lined up. Catching his breath, he paused and then stood as straight as he could, not giving Lupo a chance to fill him in on what he and Kitty had discovered in the park.

"Dear friend, dear friend . . ." the distressed mouse began. "Well, where to start, dear boy, where to start? The good news, perhaps . . . Yes, the good news . . . You have the support of the mice communities. They all believe you are innocent. That is good. I therefore have decided that I would be the best representative for you. The Grand Jury will be assembled. They will want answers, I think I have the best handle on how to help you . . . but you need to tell me everything . . ."

"Herbert, the mice are right. I am innocent."

Not listening, Herbert rambled on. "No, Lupo, let me finish. Everyone is very angry. Imperial Swans Europe-wide are calling for your expulsion from the Palace."

"But I had nothing to do with it, Herbert," he barked as loudly as he could. "I promise!"

"Paw prints and black fur were found at the crime scene, Lupo. We have to face facts – you were there. You had the swan's neck in your mouth!"

Lupo was hurt. "I *was* there but . . ." Lupo hung his head, tears pricking his dark eyes. He didn't know which was worse: being accused or being doubted by his best friend. "Herbert, this is me we are talking about. You know me. I didn't do it. Ask the squirrels, they can back me up."

"Yes, well, I did speak to Jessica and she claims that you have been bothering her for months. She says you always chased her to the Imperial Swans. She told Percy and me that she was happy she could help bring you to justice."

Then Herbert walked up to Lupo and stared into the young dog's eyes. There was no look of dishonesty, no lies hiding behind his soft but sad face. A hundred thousand mice couldn't be wrong. If they believed he was innocent then he should trust that his own instincts were right. He loved Lupo and deep down knew he was the very opposite to his bad student Vulcan. "You would tell me if you had done it, wouldn't you?" he asked.

"I promise you, Herbert, I didn't hurt Cyrus."

The little mouse burst into tears of relief. Herbert believed that he was innocent and that it was all just a matter of the royal dog being in the wrong place at the wrong time.

"Dry your eyes," Lupo smiled. "I need your help."

They all sat down in the middle of the kitchen. For some time they discussed what he had seen and their meetings with the squirrels in the park.

Herbert stood up. He walked round and round them, distracted. When they told him about Vulcan, he felt something stir inside. He had always had deep worries about Vulcan.

Back when the dorgi had been a small puppy

he had ignored the more serious lessons and only seemed to be interested in the darker animal myths and legends. They were the stories that told of beasts that ravaged humans, unimaginable treasures, terror and death.

Once Vulcan had a taste, he was relentless. Herbert recalled one afternoon telling Vulcan about the hidden passageways and long corridors beneath the palaces. It was a mistake. The dorgi spent days lost in them. Herbert vowed never to tell another pupil about them again. M.I.5 had sent so many teams out to rescue the royal dog. He had once been found half-starved and exhausted, his dorgi legs too short to carry him great distances. He had made it all the way to France using corridors that were crumbling and dangerous – unused since the French Revolution!

Banned from roaming around the corridors, Vulcan turned to books for knowledge. His thirst was unquenchable. He read great volumes, dusty and withered. He was eager to read about the most terrifying of creatures. He would ask constantly if there had ever been an animal ruler and if it was possible for an animal kingdom to rule in place of the humans.

Believing that it was just a phase and that Vulcan was just a keen student, Herbert had made the terrible mistake of telling him that nothing was impossible and that there were *"objects that had the power to change the world"*.

The dorgi had become withdrawn and unteachable from that point onwards. He was uninterested in serving loyally, the key to being a good royal dog. The myths consumed Vulcan. When he was large enough, he had attacked Herbert for not wanting to tell him how to find the treasures. Herbert had cowered behind a thick book, *"I refuse to teach you these things. They are nothing more than myths, you are delving too far into the past. Leave it where it belongs. These objects are lost in time for a good reason. Leave them be."*

"LEAVE ME," was the last thing Vulcan had said to Herbert.

Lupo could see the concern on the little mouse's face. "Vulcan is up to something," he said. "And if it has anything to do with St George and the Dragon we could all be in danger. Herbert, I need you to tell me everything you know."

Herbert pulled on his long whiskers, a habit he

had when he was thinking. "We also need to address the issue of the Grand Jury." He looked at the floor and then back at Lupo's dark face. "The Grand Jury hasn't been convened in many years. We'll have to plead your case first thing. Should we win, we'll be given two weeks to prepare for a trial. The Jury will reconvene to hear what we have to say and then it will deliver its verdict."

Lupo stood up. His blood was running hot then cold. He stared into the faces of his best friends. "What happens if I'm convicted?"

Kitty got up and walked over to her friend, putting a paw on his shoulder. "Lupo, if you are convicted, you will be sent to the Tower of London."

"The Tower of London . . . but it's a tourist attraction. Isn't it?"

"Indeed it is, but its also the worst animal prison we have." Herbert looked scared. "Lupo, you don't want to go there. Animals don't return once they go there. Conditions are positively medieval."

The courtroom was located underneath the Albert Memorial, right opposite the Albert Hall. It was HQ to Animal Law Enforcement and the Magpie Police.

The case would be heard in Court Room No.1 and the Grand Jury would be made up of seven members:

Judge No.1: A squirrel, who was widely known to not like dogs.

Judge No. 2: A mallard duck, who was as deaf as a plank of wood.

Judge No. 3: An owl, who was unused to having to be awake during the day and so kept nodding off.

Judge No. 4: An ant, who didn't like animals . . . at all.

Judge No. 5: A black beetle, so old he needed to be carried around by ladybirds.

Judge No. 6: Percy Pigeon, who had already made up his mind that Lupo was guilty.

And last, there was Judge No. 7: Cyrus's wife Marie Louise who would act on behalf of all the Imperial Swans.

Lupo was not comforted when he heard that a stone-blind earthworm would stand in if any members were unable to attend.

There was little time to prepare a defence. The evidence was damning. His paw prints were all over the crime scene. This was bad enough, but witnesses said that they had seen Lupo with Cyrus, and black

fur had been found on the broken wing.

M.I.5 mice had been quickly dispatched to re-check the scene to see if there was anything that had been missed by the magpies. They returned with a wooden box. It had been found discarded in the undergrowth. Covered in weeds, it looked like it had been underwater for many years, held down by something heavy inside it. When they opened it at HQ it was clear what had been in it. The rich red velvet interior was designed to fit a sword.

"The Sword of St George," Lupo whispered out loud. "That was what Vulcan wanted and that is what injured Cyrus."

"It can't be – the story of St George is a myth!" Herbert was astonished, then fell silent. "I told Vulcan about it . . . Oh no, this is all my fault. It was the first legend I told him about. He was obsessed with it, he craved as much knowledge as possible. 'Knowledge is power,' he kept saying. He asked me about the sword and the ring. I . . . I never thought he would go as far as to hurt another animal!"

"Well, he figured it all out, that's for sure. We need to find out what he learnt. Vulcan had to have found a book or a map or something that told him he needed the Sword of Ascalon."

"The library," said Herbert nervously.

Lupo heard the fear in his friend's voice, "Which library?"

Herbert knew that time was not on their side and it was a long shot. "I think we need to go to Windsor Castle – the library there is full of ancient royal myths and legends. St George's chapel is also there. I think we may have the best chance of finding the answers we seek if we go to Windsor."

Lupo agreed. "Whatever Vulcan discovered was important. There is a lot more to that fable than we all think. Vulcan needed that sword. I need to find out more about that sword and what it means." He looked at his friend. "Herbert, I can't go to Windsor – everyone is watching me. I barely got out of the palace."

"There is a way, but it's risky," answered Herbert "We can go tonight. Everyone is distracted and if we leave it till late we should have enough time to get there and find what we need and get back before they even notice you are gone."

Herbert paused, and looked at his old wristwatch. "I'd better be off or I will be late." Gathering his papers together he said his goodbyes. "The Grand Jury will be in shortly. Keep your paws crossed that we get the time we need to investigate." And off he went in the direction of the memorial. The entrance was between Prince Albert's golden feet.

Right on the dot of nine o'clock, the judges entered the sacred space inside the memorial. Lupo was not required to attend but agreed to meet his friend outside the courts in the park afterwards.

Herbert walked in solemnly and, after greeting the Grand Jury, he called his first witness – the squirrel who had been chased by Lupo that fateful morning.

Jessica darted into the room nervously. "He's guilty! I tell you! Guilty!" It was no good. Jessica's lies filled the room.

The court erupted into a frenzy. Order had to be called and after a short fruit-and-nut break, the Grand Jury retook their seats.

A second witness, a young duck, cried non-stop as she explained that whatever attacked Cyrus was able to swim and hold its breath for a great deal of time.

A hearing was hastily arranged for two weeks'

time, when the judges would rule on the evidence provided by both sides.

Walking out of the courtroom, Herbert felt like he had failed his friend. He met up with Lupo. They sat together next to a park bench. Nanny had tied the new chain lead to the side of the buggy, so that there was no chance of Lupo escaping. She sang as, contentedly, she rocked the young Prince whilst feeding him carrot sticks.

"I'm sorry it's not better news. I was hoping it would be over, but it isn't," explained Herbert.

Lupo was even more determined to uncover the truth. "We'll go tonight to Windsor. You're right – everyone is so distracted that this just might be the only chance we get. How do we get there?"

"We have to take the Blue route – its hidden entrance is within the ancient wine cellar at Kensington Palace. Meet me there at midnight."

Lupo explained the plan to Kitty who offered to hide under Lupo's blanket in his bed within the kitchen so that no one would notice his disappearance if they came looking for him. She also gave him one of George's uncle's handkerchiefs. Within it was a cheese sandwich for Herbert and a sausage from someone's breakfast.

"It's not much, but it's a long way to Windsor," she said. "Good luck."

Herbert whistled and a small group of mice dragged an old apple sack over to Lupo. "You had better put that on. I doubt we shall see anyone who recognizes you but just in case."

Lupo ripped the sack into a cloak and tied it around his head. His handsome face was now shielded from any prying or inquisitive eyes.

They found the entrance to the Blue route between a rack of two-hundred-year-old red wine and one of gently ageing champagne. Like all the routes this one had been designed to protect the royal family from both the weather and peasant mobs, giving them a clean and comfortable route to Windsor Castle.

The years passed and the urban animals jostled for homes within the City, while the royal family forgot their routes and abandoned their clever passages. So the animals had moved in.

Lupo noticed that the Blue route was long and fairly wide. Herbert warned him to "Duck under your hood a bit deeper if we see any sparrows. They are the lamplighters and the unofficial guardians of this route. If they see us they will surely report us to the magpies."

After several miles it was clear that Herbert was struggling to keep up. Lupo gently scooped the little mouse up in his paws and plonked him on to the back of his neck. He said, "I really appreciate everything that you are doing for me, Herbert. The least I can do is give you a lift to Windsor Castle."

Herbert didn't object. Lupo's large paws and longer legs gave him a distinct advantage: mice can be fast but, on the whole, they are unused to having to travel long distances. Grateful as he was for the lift, however, he was equally unhappy about the comfort of his ride.

They came to a section of the route that was blocked by a large oak. The old tree had buried itself deep within the passageway. They had no choice but to climb down the branches and into the City of Creatures far below.

"Once we are on the other side we can climb back up to re-join the Blue route. Just be careful," said Herbert nervously. "The City is no place for an animal like you. Head down and eyes forward. OK?"

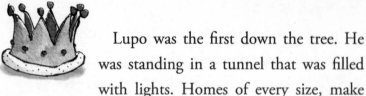 Lupo was the first down the tree. He was standing in a tunnel that was filled with lights. Homes of every size, make and model were piled high along the tunnel. Wood, paper, tin and old bottles sheltered foxes, rabbits, black and white mice and rats. The City's tunnel was an important home and road through London for the urban animals but thankfully, there seemed to be few around.

Lupo peeked in to an old jam jar and saw a family of mice sleeping one on top of the other. The City of Creatures occupants were unaware the famous royal dog was walking amongst their humble dwellings.

It took some time but they eventually found a way around the tree. Herbert eagerly leaped on to a branch to begin the climb back up to the Blue route. He was keen to get them out of the City before being spotted.

As they made their way back up the tree, Lupo could hear the sparrow guardians twittering about the day's events. It was clear to him that many of the tiny birds had made their minds up. "Lupo's guilty!" they cried as they swooped in and out of their nests.

Herbert was listening, too. He climbed down,

jumping back on to the back of Lupo's neck. "Don't worry, dear chap," he said. "They may illuminate the way ahead, but they can't shed light on this case. We should stop soon. I need a break."

Lupo was panting now. They had been travelling for over three hours. His paws were sore and his neck stiff from carrying the bundle of food and the little mouse. They stopped just outside of London.

The Blue route overhead showed that they were halfway to Windsor. The walls around them were covered in wax from candles that had spilt over the centuries. There was an overflow pipe that dropped into a stone watering hole. Usually this was where animals collected the water for their homes and businesses. Tonight it was where Lupo rested his weary paws. The lights above were further apart, making it easier to hide from bats flying overhead looking for insects.

Lupo gave Herbert the cheese sandwich. He was too tired to eat. His mind was ticking over, trying to solve the mysterious attack on Cyrus. "The duck said that the murderer acted in the middle of the night, right?"

"Yes, awful watching a duck crying like that,"

replied the mouse, crumbs falling as he nibbled the sandwich.

"The thing I just don't understand is what Cyrus was doing on the lake? He had to have been guarding the sword." Lupo felt a slight twitching in his tail. "Whoever the murderer was had to be a strong swimmer and small enough to get in and out of the water without making too much noise."

Herbert took a mouthful of cheese. "Indeed, I was thinking about the black fur found on the wing. That rules out Vulcan. He must have had help."

"It could have been a rat: the squirrel in the park said that a buck rat had delivered all the nuts from Buckingham Palace," said Lupo.

"We need evidence, but you could be right. A rat would be small and quiet enough, even strong enough to attack Cyrus." Herbert finished his sandwich and both of them looked up at the ceiling to see how far they had to travel. Painted deer leaped over the Blue line. They didn't have much further.

Lupo pictured Holly's face for a second and said, "Do you think Holly will be at Windsor?"

"Yes, the Queen is in residence, so we will have to be extra careful. Vulcan is sure to be there too,"

Herbert replied.

Lupo growled.

Lightening the mood, Herbert offered, "Holly just won first place at the International Dog Show. She is such a beauty, and her manners smite me – first rate. The royal family is so proud. Why did you ask about her – do you think she is in on it too?"

"No, no, Holly I trust. She's different," replied Lupo, staring down the corridor. Picturing her face, he forgot about his sore paws and heavy legs.

Holly was wagging her tail, waiting for them at the less grand lower entrance to Windsor Castle. The entrance was through a neglected linen cupboard in an unused and dilapidated servants' dining hall.

"Herbert, it's always a pleasure to see you. Your colleagues in Mice Intelligence alerted me to your imminent arrival." Shyly, she looked over to Lupo, and batted her long eyelashes a couple of times. "Hello, Lupo."

Lupo stared as if caught in a wonderful dream. Herbert nudged him back to life.

"I managed to slip away," she said, blushing.

Holly had left the Queen sleeping in the yellow

bedroom with Willow. Only Vulcan had stirred as she had snuck out of the room. But many of the guards had retired for the night, so it was easy for her to run through the castle to greet them on time.

"Bertie told me you might be coming," she said. "I think he's been quite taken with you since you freed him from that coal bucket. He is a good friend to me, so thank you."

Lupo smiled, glad that Bertie was safe from Kitty's games at Kensington Palace – and even gladder he'd inadvertently pleased Holly.

Holly's fine blonde coat was gleaming it was so clean. Sniffing the air around her he noted a hint of rose. It made his tummy go funny with happiness.

"The Queen was deeply saddened about the attack on Cyrus," Holly said. "She herself protects the swans. The attack really did unnerve her. I don't think I have ever seen her so shaken up about an animal before. She wants to see the Duke and Duchess. They will all decide if you should remain in the palace. If Her Majesty thinks you are guilty she will tell them that you need to be removed." She looked down at the ground, her own fears unravelling. "Do you have any idea who did it?"

"Afraid not, Holly. Lupo and I are on our way to the archives," Herbert replied. "We have some clues, but, as yet, no answers."

The elegant corgi stared sadly at them both. She hesitated, and a string of tears filled her large eyes. "I want to help, if I can. I couldn't bear it if you ended up being locked up at the Tower."

Lupo didn't think it was fair to drag her into his nightmare, but he wasn't in a position to refuse her support. "Holly, I need all the help I can get at the moment. Thank you for being here." He was bashful all of a sudden. "It means a lot," he added.

Holly was swift to change the subject. "We'd better get to the archives. What is it that you are looking for anyway?"

Lupo proceeded to explain. Holly listened, shocked and saddened. "Do you really think St George existed?"

"Yes. I think he was as much alive as you or me," replied Lupo.

Holly looked afraid. "So if you think he was alive then what about the . . ."

"And the dragon too."

Holly's blonde ears flicked left then right – a sure

119

sign she was uncomfortable. "But that's . . . it's . . . impossible. Dragons aren't real."

"Why wouldn't they be? Before us, there were dinosaurs. Why not dragons?" questioned Herbert.

Holly wasn't convinced. "Yes I know but, fire-breathing, talon-scratching dragons?"

"You're forgetting maiden-eating!" interjected Herbert, almost instantly regretting what he said. Holly looked genuinely scared.

Lupo dared to comfort her by resting one of his paws on hers. "Holly, if there is a dragon, it is probably long dead. I mean the story is hundreds of years old. Dragons can't live that long."

"Oh yes they can," Herbert interrupted. "The humans have yet to see the super-sized crocodiles that swim along the bottom of the Thames . . . Only last week—" Seeing their reactions he stopped. "I've done it again . . . said too much, argh! Here we are. Follow this staircase up and we should pop out right in the middle of the archives."

The Royal Archives were "Closed for Cleaning."

Herbert finished scribbling the note and bolted off to stick it in the window. Flicking on the main lights

120

with his tail, he hoped that no one would suspect anything. After all, it was the middle of the night.

Herbert crawled into a desk near the entrance and was able to locate the keys so that he could unlock a series of old cabinets and cupboards containing rare books. They walked around large bookcases and pointed at them, occasionally sneezing as thick yellow dust whisked around their paws.

"Dusty, isn't it?" said Lupo, coughing and sneezing.

Herbert brushed himself off. "We are in the part of the archives that no one bothers with much. It's next to impossible to get in here. You need all sorts of special permissions and passes if you are a human. Sad to think they know so little about the treasures littered just about everywhere."

"One day you and I need to have a serious chat about all this treasure you keep mentioning," Lupo muttered as he scanned the library books for anything that might be of importance.

Herbert scaled a ladder and began flicking through some books. "Years ago I saw a report on conditions within these archives. A few mice had begun to make it their home. No good came of that, let me tell you.

Never seen so many reports of broken bones, thanks to traps. So watch out, this place is booby-trapped! I'm going to see if I can find the book, which should lead me to a small animal archive. Only I can't recall which one it is . . . let me think . . ." Herbert was darting along the tops of the books high above them. "That's a good place for me to start. I want to see if there is any evidence of a dragon existing outside of stories." Suddenly he jumped for joy. "*All Creatures Great and Small!* That's it! That's the book I need to crawl behind!"

Holly and Lupo watched as he dashed over a few books and was gone.

"Looks like it's just the two of us," said Holly, shyly.

"Holly, thanks for this. I know it can't have been easy getting away," said Lupo, seeing her sweet blushes.

"Well, it's not every day I get to go on an adventure. I was thinking about what you said when we first met. You said I must have lots of adventures in the Palace. Truth is, Lupo, I really haven't. As a royal dog I have orders I have to follow, you know?"

Lupo was staring at her strangely.

"What's wrong?" she asked.

"Holly! THAT'S IT!"

Holly was confused. "What's it?"

"Royal Orders, that's what we need to find! Cyrus drew the Shield of St George into the ground. The Royal Order of Ascalon has the St George's Shield as its insignia. That is what Cyrus was trying to tell us. He was pointing us to the Royal Order of Ascalon." Lupo's tail hadn't wagged as much in days. "The Duke's a member – he has the insignia in his office! It was right there staring me in the face, Holly."

Holly was relieved. "Fantastic! Now we are on to something. I'm going to see if I can find anything about the Order."

"Right! Go for it . . . I'm going to—" he turned around and she was gone. He muttered to himself, "I'm going to stand here like a lemon and – LUPO, pull yourself together. She is just a corgi . . ."

"What?" asked Holly, reappearing behind a book. "Did you say something?"

"No! No! Nothing . . . now where's that book on swords I was looking for?" Embarrassed, he ducked behind a bookcase. "We should also keep a look out for anything relating to St George."

Holly hid her smiles behind a pile of books. "Why St George?"

Lupo walked around the bookcase and ended up face-to-face with her. "Because, St George is the Patron Saint of England. He is normally depicted with the shield."

She nodded. "OK."

"Thanks, Holly."

"It's now as much my adventure as yours. It's me who should be thanking you, Lupo," she said, smiling into his eyes.

A grandfather clock chimed loudly; it was midnight. All alone, Lupo managed to read several books, none of which even bothered to mention St George. As he settled before another weighty volume, dawn's pale light filtered through snowflakes that had gathered in the corners of the large windows. A series of loud, excited barks suddenly ruptured the silence. He had found something. It didn't take Holly or Herbert long to get to him.

"What is it?" asked Herbert, huffing and puffing, out of breath from running over several bookcases.

"*The Ancient Order of Ascalon and its Ceremonies*," said Lupo, clutching the book with both paws. "Guys, I think I have found something interesting. Look at this."

Carefully he opened the book. The shield of St George filled the first page. It was white with a red cross in the centre and surrounded by a roaring dragon. Alongside the shield was a sword.

Pointing at it, Lupo spoke slowly, "That is the Sword of Ascalon and that shield represents the Order of Ascalon. It dates back hundreds of years. No one really knows how it all started but it says here that only the bravest and the most noble knights were given the honour of being included within the Order. There's more – every year, the Order is celebrated in a private ceremony here at Windsor."

Lupo looked at Herbert. "Herbert, you told me that the Order was a mixture of animals and humans. Didn't you also tell me that there was a group of unknown animal knights?"

Herbert was curious. "I did, yes, but unfortunately, no one has ever discovered who those knights were and, besides, the order is so old I doubt these so-called knights still exist. Certainly, no animals attend the ceremony with the Queen. I mean, it would be ridiculous. An animal in the middle of St George's Chapel with the Queen of England."

"What if there were animal knights but they were called something different . . . like . . . Imperial Swans." Lupo's large brown eyes were wide with hope.

"That's it! Lupo! That's it." Herbert danced from one foot to the other.

"I am willing to bet my life on it that there is something in the chapel that will confirm my suspicions," said Lupo.

"I don't understand. Are we saying that Cyrus was a Knight of the Realm and was a member of the Order of Ascalon?" asked Holly.

Herbert had stopped dancing.

Lupo sat on the floor alongside the book. His left paw was touching the powerful symbols laid out on the page below. Everything felt like it made sense, but somehow the pieces of the jigsaw were yet to come together. He was trying to figure out a great big ancient puzzle.

His friends waited. All three of them were now

looking at the dragon, wrapped around the Shield of St George.

At last Lupo spoke. "Cyrus had to have been protecting the Sword of Ascalon. It had to have been at the bottom of the lake for hundreds of years."

"That's it! We're on a quest – just like the Knights of the Realm," said Herbert, sitting down on the floor next to Lupo. He rubbed his forehead and squinted at the spaniel through tired eyes.

"That's all very well . . ." Holly said, sneezing. "But knights fight things, and I think we already have enough of a battle on our hands just trying to save you from the Grand Jury." Sunlight was beginning to fill the room. She looked at the tired friends. "I have to get going, Her Majesty will be up early to go riding."

"Cyrus pointed us to the Shield of St George," Lupo continued. "I think that means he was trying to warn the Order and that is why he told me to 'protect the secret'. The Order of Ascalon hides a secret. It has to be a pretty big one and Vulcan has discovered it."

He couldn't hide his thoughts from her any longer. She needed to know that they suspected

Vulcan was to blame for everything.

But Holly went very pale. "Vulcan has nothing to do with this . . . does he? I mean he can't – he's Her Majesty's favourite dog. He can't be involved. He's asleep upstairs." She was confused and concerned.

Lupo spoke softly back to her. "Holly, I'm sorry we didn't tell you. We think he is involved."

"You are wrong. You've gone too far. I'm leaving. Good night." Holly turned to walk out.

Lupo shouted after her, "Please, Holly I need your help! Vulcan has somehow got his paws on the truth and he has the Sword of Ascalon. Don't you see? If he has the sword and he is here, then the secret is here at Windsor Castle."

It was too late; she was gone. A cloud of dust scattered in the air as she slammed the doorway to the corridor.

10
The Clock That
Doesn't Tick

It had been a week since they had returned from
Windsor. Inspecting the pads on the bottom of his
paws, Lupo saw that he had a large blister in between
his claws. He licked it, hoping it would heal soon.
Looking up, he heard two gardeners slipping on the
frozen ground outside the nursery window. It was
the first time in what felt like days that he had been
let into the nursery. George had particularly missed
him at nights.

"*Dodo! Dodo!*" gurgled Prince George, happy to
see his friend.

Lupo crawled under the big cot and told George
that he had been gone so long because he was trying
to find the dragon. He told George all about his trip
to Windsor Castle. The Prince loved hearing about

the winding passageway along the Blue route and all the animal homes.

George was very quiet when Lupo told him about Vulcan. "Bad dog!" the young Prince frowned.

"Yes, exactly," Lupo sighed.

Nanny walked into the room, "GET OUT, LUPO!" her hand gesturing towards the kitchen, "BED!"

The Duchess just happened to be walking down the hallway when she saw Lupo low to the ground, dashing back to his bed in the kitchen. She followed him. "Oh dear, you poor thing. What on earth are we going to do with you? I just can't believe you did something so dreadful. RSPCA inspectors want to come and see me. They want us to send you away. Lupo, I couldn't bear to lose you."

Her long brown hair dangled in his face and one of her tears rolled off her cheek and on to his nose.

"Any word from Herbert?" Lupo asked a palace mouse as it tried to wedge itself through a gap in the kitchen cabinets with a cube of sugar.

"Nope!" it shouted back.

Kitty was reclining in the rocking chair, gently

swinging. "He'll come when he can. You just hang in there. Watching you is like watching the kettle boil."

"I know, Kitty, you're right. I was hoping that we would have news by now. I need to get back to Windsor Castle. I want to investigate the Chapel of St George. There has to be something in there that confirms the Imperial Swans are part of the Order of Ascalon."

"You know the way out – just go and check it out!"

"I can't, Kitty. Herbert says that it's best I stay here until he can ensure some kind of protection for me. Apparently the animals are baying for my blood."

"I'm not going to lie – it's pretty bad out there. George's uncle was watching the news last night with me – and I am telling you, even the news channels in Hong Kong are talking about you. Out there it is *much* worse. Animals want to know why you haven't been sent to the Tower already."

The following day there *was* news. Herbert appeared in the living room, having run down the satellite wires, carrying Lupo's case file in his left hand. In the hope of working out how Cyrus was connected to the Order of Ascalon, he'd been spending more and more time at the Queen's London residence. "You were right," he declared. "There's more to the Imperial Swans than meets the eye."

Kitty's ears pricked up and she stopped playing with Nanny's ball of wool. She kicked it into the Duchess's open handbag on the floor of the living room. A picture of Lupo and Prince George fell out of one of the pockets.

"Cyrus's wife, Marie Louise, has reviewed my evidence and has asked me to meet her today," said Herbert. "I think she may confirm that Cyrus was involved in the Order."

"Any word from Holly?" Lupo asked hopefully.

"Yes, indeed. But I have other news, old chap. According to the Queen's schedule the entire family is due to travel to Windsor on Friday for a state dinner. The Duke and Duchess are attending. The Queen has suggested that you join them. I think she wants to see if you are capable of causing trouble. So whatever you do at Windsor, remember to keep your head down. One whiff of trouble and that will be it. The Queen will not abide badly-behaved animals. I shall see you there. Oh, better not forget.

Holly asked me to give you this." Opening the case file, Herbert pulled out an envelope with "Lupo" written on the front.

"What is it?" Lupo took the envelope.

"I'm sorry, I don't know, but she said she wanted you to have it before the weekend. I guess she has forgiven us for not telling her we think Vulcan's responsible."

Lupo eyes scanned the tiny envelope and he ran his nose along the back of it. The envelope smelled of summer's garden roses, a scent he often noticed lingering around Holly.

Kitty kicked the photograph back into the bag with her paw. It was her cue to chime in. "HA! I knew it. Lupo likes Holly, Lupo likes Holly!"

Suppressing a smile, Herbert ignored her – and focused on the clock on the mantelpiece. "Good gracious! I must be going. I don't want to be late for Marie Louise – we need that confirmation. See you at Windsor."

"It's safe for me to travel then?"

"No, but we need to get on – we only have a week left before the trial. Meet me at the Chapel of St George. On Friday night it's the annual animal meeting. It's an *Announcement Service*. Very special stuff and it's the excuse we need to get you into the chapel. Gives you a chance to have a look around."

"Thank you, Herbert and . . ." Before Lupo could say goodbye, the mouse was off – squeezing his way through a gap in the tiles alongside the fireplace. Hearing the back door to the kitchen open, Kitty left too.

Alone, Lupo retreated to a corner to open Holly's envelope. A card was inside. On the front was a picture of Windsor Castle covered in snow – and inside was a paw-written note.

Dearest Lupo,

I think you are right about V. I'm so sorry I doubted you.

You still have my support.

Holly

X

He didn't know what had swayed her opinion.

All he knew was that he was glad to have her on side once again. He would need it if he would avoid getting into trouble at Windsor.

That night, Prince George was particularly fretful. Without Lupo under his cot to calm him, he cried endlessly.

Lupo was desperate to go to the royal baby. He could hear the sound of footsteps padding up and down the corridor between the Duke and Duchess's room and the nursery – at one o'clock and again at three and finally at four o'clock. It eventually became too much for him. Concerned about George's restlessness, Lupo carefully made it to the nursery hoping not to bump into Nanny.

To his surprise he found the Duke singing gently to his son, soothing him to sleep. Lupo watched; his heart would surely break if he was taken away from George.

Too upset to carry on watching them, he went to the Duke's office. No one ever looked for him in here. Settling by the dying embers of a fire he glanced up at the many silver-framed photographs of the royal family.

"Vulcan won't win," he said to himself. He was filled with a new determination.

As the royal cars were loaded for the journey to Windsor, Lupo looked back at Kitty, worried that she would be on her own at Kensington Palace. He reminded himself that the cat knew how to take care of herself.

A bodyguard offered to take him for a quick walk and, passing through the gates, Percy flapped down from his perch. "Don't think for a second I believe that report Herbert has sent around. I know you are guilty! I can feel it in my bones!"

"Report?" Lupo replied.

"That Marie Louise thinks you are innocent – something about you being in the wrong place and the wrong time! Humph, like I think *that's* true!" Percy was clearly annoyed. His head bobbed up and down furiously. "You may be holed up in that castle but I will make sure I have daily reports on your activity – any funny business, and the Grand Jury will hear of it! Herbert is not the only one who can write a report, you know."

The priggish pigeon was interrupted by the

bodyguard's radio. The royal family was ready for the off. For once, Lupo was glad to be denied a walk.

As the car's wheels rolled over the cobbled stones of Windsor Castle, Lupo felt a sudden, inexplicable surge of excitement. Out of the back of the car, he saw tourists and a large group of children lining up to go into the public.

When the gates closed behind the car, they entered the Lower Ward and drove slowly past St George's Chapel. Then, as they drove up the hill towards the Upper Ward, he saw a red postbox and some cottages. A ceremonial Queen's Guard saluted as they passed.

The car eventually came to a stop beneath a covered archway, and palace staff rushed out to help unload and to shake hands with their co-workers. While everyone busied themselves with the unpacking, Lupo slipped through the main door and took a good look around.

The contrast with the Queen's London residence was stark. While Buckingham Palace was welcoming and grand, Windsor felt mysterious and imposing. Every corridor was carpeted in red. There were swords and shields on the walls, and flags and banners. He made his way to through the ancient armoury.

"Can I help you?" enquired Vulcan, sitting on King Henry VIII's throne. He made his presence felt – like a slap in the face.

Lupo felt his heart beat faster, adrenalin rushing through his body. The sight of the evil dog revolted him. The royal dorgi had caused so much anguish and pain to so many. Lupo fought every urge to question Vulcan, to ask him "Why?" His voice was shaky and when he opened his mouth to speak, what came out was a soft but deep growl, his anger unmistakable. "Vulcan." At the same moment he was feeling all the pain Vulcan's action had caused. George's sweet face came into his thoughts, instantly calming him down. This was not the time nor the place to engage with Vulcan.

"Lupo, a pleasure to see you. I was hoping you would come. You may bow, if you like." Vulcan flashed a look of annoyance. "Lupo – you may address

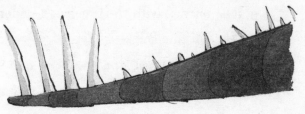

139

me with either Your Highness or sir."

"What?" Lupo gripped the red carpet beneath his black paws with frustration.

"You will learn, *pup*, to respect your elders. I suggest you learn fast. I hear the Duke and Duchess are discussing your future away from Kensington Palace. Future looks grim for you, doesn't it? Shame . . . and I thought you and I would be such good friends." Vulcan stood up in his throne and looked down at Lupo.

It was all too much. The dorgi's dark eyes bored into Lupo's own, searching for a reaction. Vulcan wanted Lupo to lose his temper, to lash out. But Lupo held his nerve. He had to stay out of trouble. He tried to think about Holly and Herbert. He did not want to let his friends down. At the same time he needed Vulcan to know that he hadn't got away with it all.

"I know you did it, Vulcan. Your paws are all over it," he said, baring his teeth for an instant and almost immediately regretting it. It was exactly what Vulcan wanted.

"Temper, temper, don't want to end up on that nasty chain leash again do we . . . ? Stuck in the castle kitchen instead of your beloved Kensington Palace. Dreadfully cold place, this one. No – attacking me is not a good idea. I suggest you hold your tongue. Have a good stay, Lupo. Oh, one last thing—" The corgi got down and, circling the spaniel, inspected him as though he were a teenage soldier on parade. "We, that is the family and I, will be gathering in the main drawing room for drinks before the animals leave to attend the Announcement Service in St George's Chapel. Your presence is not required at the drinks, but please refrain from being late to the service. We do not condone tardiness here at the castle." As a final note, he jumped on to Henry's VIII's priceless footstool near the throne, before coming nose-to-nose with Lupo. "Are we understood?" Vulcan's mouth curled into an evil smile on one side of his face.

Lupo had already been lured into one of Vulcan's traps. He forced himself to keep his mouth closed, knowing that bullies never win and that Vulcan's time was coming.

"Good – very good." Vulcan had what he wanted. Lupo seemed to be unable to speak. He could hear something around the corner. "Oh,

Holly, for heaven's sake, come in. I can hear your dreadful panting!"

Holly appeared at the entrance, and instantly Lupo felt more at ease. Subdued by Vulcan's tone, she moved sedately towards them. "Hello, Lupo." She seemed nervous, but her eyes sparkled in a way that made Lupo's stomach flip flop.

Vulcan commanded, "Please show Lupo around. It is your job to ensure that he doesn't get into any trouble whilst he is here. I would so hate it if things got . . . quarrelsome."

Both Holly and Lupo watched in relief as Vulcan trotted off in the direction of the grand staircase.

"Who does he think he is?" said Lupo, as soon as Vulcan was out of earshot.

"A King, I'm afraid. Perhaps even, *the* King," answered Holly. She moved closer, whispering, "You'll never guess," she began, her voice lowered. "A couple of years ago, he tried to get a load of the palace animals to sign up to the *Vulcan Army*, saying that all of us animals *needed to stick together* and that one day our time would come and . . . oh, for ages he went on. Pitched to everyone at the Announcement Service in the Chapel."

"You're kidding!" Lupo was aghast.

"No, I'm not. Deadly serious, I'm afraid."

"Did anyone join up?" he asked.

"Oh yes, quite a few I believe," said Holly. "He pretends he's the loyal servant of the crown, but deep down he thinks he's as good as the Queen. I really do believe that. I'm sorry I doubted your judgement. I've been watching him and he's up to something. He's been disappearing every night. Try as I might, I haven't been able to follow him."

"Holly, you must be careful. If Vulcan catches you, he might hurt you." Lupo wasn't afraid to show her how he felt.

Holly replied confidently, "Vulcan wouldn't hurt me. He wouldn't dare."

Lupo saw a flash of strength glimmer behind her eyes. She changed the subject promptly. "Anyway, how about that tour? This place is amazing – beheaded ghosts, priceless objects, trusted stallions . . . oh, and a great fire . . ."

Lupo and Holly chatted whilst touring the grand old castle. When they arrived at the Horseshoe Cloister in the Lower Ward they realized they had almost completely lost track of time. Ten of the

Queen's most gallant horses walked with both reverence and supremacy towards the chapel.

"Hurry up, Lupo!" Holly cried. "If they are heading in, then we are late!"

Candlelight bathed St George's Chapel. Hundreds of palace animals were gathered together in neat packs along a chequered white-and-black tiled floor. No one spoke. Everyone remained silent in homage to the ancient building. Once a year they were allowed in, and this year the turnout had been particularly big, thanks to a boom in the palace's mouse and rabbit populations.

Holly suspected everyone wanted a glimpse of Lupo, "the Accused". As she guided her friend through the magpies that were guarding the entrance, the silence was suspiciously broken.

"The guilty is here!" a small group of active sparrows chanted.

"Why is Holly with that wretched dog?" shouted a lone wolf.

"The Grand Jury will convict!" squeaked a badger.

Lupo tried hard not to take too much notice, but it wasn't easy. His eyes caught sight of a tiny mouse. He watched as she dived inside the pocket of her

mother's apron.

Holly could sense Lupo's courage. "Please ignore them," she whispered. "They don't know what they are talking about. Anyway, the bishop will soon be here to put a stop to it all."

For days, Holly had been doing her best to defend her friend and clear his name. During a birthday party for a Butler Badger at the Queen's doll's house, she'd attempted to persuade animals of his innocence. But Fat Boy Slime (who had travelled in from the garden shed to perform) demanded she give back the microphone – and she couldn't compete with his thumping beats.

Now, looking at the lovably unkempt Lupo at her side, she vowed she'd do anything she could to help him. Gently, she tilted her head towards his and directed him to a pew.

To distract himself, Lupo turned his gaze up towards the banners hanging brightly in the candlelight from the ceiling. "Holly," he whispered, "what are those?"

"The banners of the Order of Ascalon," she replied, shushing him.

Lupo was transfixed. Hand-sewn silk displayed

knights' colours. Stars, a raven, crosses and even a red rose were used to proudly identify the brave few who had been awarded the highest honour. One banner had been removed and was resting against the wall. It was a banner of a swan and St George's shield. Lupo could not contain himself. Forgetting where he was, he barked, "Holly! Look! Cyrus had a banner! The Shield of St George . . . look, *there* it is. That's it! It was taken down because—" Fearing the worst, he searched her eyes for an answer.

"Lupo, Cyrus's brother, will be sworn in tonight as the newest member of the Imperial Swans," said Holly. "Cyrus is still not awake. I'm sorry."

Lupo felt his heart crunch in his chest. Poor Cyrus.

With much tut-tutting and sighing, members of the congregation turned around to stare at the disgraced dog. Lupo fell silent and crouched down low on a prayer cushion at his feet.

After what seemed like minutes, but was probably just seconds, Holly nudged him. "Here comes the Bishop. Arise."

Everyone stood and watched as a bat of uncommon size dropped from the ceiling and landed in a perfect swoosh on a black tile. Looking down at the tile, it changed its mind and jumped awkwardly onto a white tile. The batty bishop had a tuft of grey hair standing upright on his head.

Opening his mouth and revealing a few too many gaps and a set of yellow teeth, he spat very unceremoniously into his hand, which was at the end of a hole-ridden pair of wings. Using a long finger, he down smoothed the offending hair. Smiling, he drew a large breath of air, yawned and smacked his gums together, lost in his own thoughts. Then, remembering where he was, he began to speak.

"Welcome everyone!" Looking around, he noticed a few friendly faces so he waved as if on stage in front of thousands of adoring fans. "Excuse me for taking a moment to bring those of you who are new up to speed. Welcome to Windsor Castle and our annual meeting. We have a few rules, which I would ask you to follow:

No chasing each other.

No eating each other.

No fighting each other.

"Now that we are all settled, we can begin. Everyone is required to elect one representative."

One by one, the representatives stood forward. When it got to Herbert's turn, Lupo's tail wagged at the sight of his friend.

"I believe Maggie represents the Magpies, Polly the Park Ranger Parrots, Rupert the Queen's Horses, Sam the Rabbits, Vulcan the Royal Dogs and Herbert Mice Intelligence Section 5, etc," the bishop continued. "Much like last year, is that right? Now, do any of the representatives have anything they wish to say to us all?"

"I have an announcement," said a small wood beetle, dressed in a slightly over-the-top ceremonial soldier's outfit.

"Yes, Major Beetle Tomlinson, please make the announcement on behalf of the insects."

The little beetle then stood as tall as he could on two legs and puffed out his chest so that everyone could make out his plummy little voice. "It has been brought to our attention that someone is 'playing' with the organ clock in the middle of the night. It is generally very disturbing. I have spoken with the mice, and they are also fed up. Last night was ridiculous. Someone was playing at two, then at four and then lastly at six forty-five! Everyone knows that this item is part the Royal Collection, and it is extremely valuable. So whoever is doing it, please desist. The organ clock is not a toy. Thank you."

Holly looked quizzical. "That's a bit odd," she said. "No one has touched that clock for years; everyone knows how valuable it is. Besides, you need the Ring of St George to play it, and last I heard it was lost."

"The Ring of St George . . ." Lupo repeated, deep in thought. "Who'd be up in the middle of the night playing with an old clock? What's so special about it?"

Holly lowered her voice so as not to disturb the Bishop, who had decided it was time for a hymn. While the entire animal congregation began to sing "*All Creatures Great and Small . . . All things wise and wonderful . . .*" she told her friend what she knew.

"It plays ten specially commissioned tunes. Last time I heard one of them was on the radio in the Queen's study."

"Sounds like we need to get a look at this clock. Is it easy to find?"

"It's in the Upper Ward, part of the public viewing area, in the state apartments – so not so easy to get to, and that's the other thing that's odd. Whoever is playing with it is risking getting into serious trouble. Every night the state rooms are patrolled by human guards. There are laser alarms and everything."

"So whoever is playing with the clock has the ring and also knows how to get around the castle without disturbing the guards," said Lupo.

The announcements were coming to an end. The batty bishop requested that everyone leave in an orderly fashion so as to avoid a stampede. By the time Lupo found Herbert, it was getting late. He had to resist the urge to jump on the small mouse, such was his excitement. "Any news?" he blurted out.

"Well, yes, dear boy, as it happens . . . I met with Marie Louise, Cyrus's wife, and it turns out we were right – there's a lot more to this."

"That's good!"

Herbert fiddled with his glasses and pushed them firmly into position on his nose. "This is highly sensitive information, old boy. The swan told me that Cyrus was on the lake for a reason."

"I knew it! He was standing guard, wasn't he? Protecting the Ascalon Sword."

"Not half. Like his father and his father's father

and his father's father's father and his father's father's father's father. They were protecting something that had been thrown into the bottom of the pond. Something of significance."

"Didn't they know it was the Sword of Ascalon?"

"No. The Imperial Swans didn't know exactly what they were guarding – only that a King's knight had asked then to protect the pond from invasion or harm. In return, they were for ever to be protected by the Crown. They were given a ring. The inscription read, 'to be worn by every animal that protects the legend that lies beneath the waters.' The swans agreed. From then on, every swan that guarded the waters wore the ring, and they became known as the Imperial Swans and were given the honour of being members of the Order of Ascalon, for services to their King and country."

Lupo raised his head again. They were back on track. "And I bet that ring is now missing," he interrupted.

"Yes, that's right. How'd you know that, my humble young hound?"

"Holly and I were just talking about the lost Ring of St George. Can it be the same ring? Do you think it's possible that they were both taken by Cyrus's attacker?"

"It makes sense that the attacker took both," said Herbert. "They were both in the Hidden Pond and they're both part of the legend of St George and the dragon."

"Holly and I think the ring is being used to work an old clock," said Lupo. "You need it to play music." Lupo looked into Herbert's eyes, convinced he was on to a major piece of the puzzle.

"Sounds a bit odd to me, Lupo," said Herbert. "A musical clock? Hardly sounds like you could do much damage with a clock? There is nothing in the fable about a clock. Are you sure?"

"I'm sure it's important," Lupo said. "There is only one way to find out. I am going to investigate the clock tonight." He looked at the mice all walking two by two towards an entrance to the kitchens. "I have a plan and I need all the mice we can get. I need a big distraction. Any chance some of your cousins can help?"

Holly, who had been talking to Major Beetle Tomlinson in the courtyard, returned. "Season's Greetings, Herbert, good to see you!" she cried. "I've just been talking to the insects' rep. That clock is definitely working. Someone is using it, Lupo. I don't think that ring is lost after all!"

The three adventurers smiled broadly at each other, united in a rush of excitement. "This is it," said Lupo. "Get in close, this is what we have to do . . ."

11
Gordon's Bible

Kensington Palace was too quiet after Lupo left for Windsor Castle. Kitty had tried to chase a few mice for excitement but found that she was too worried about Lupo to care much if she caught them.

Kitty decided to make her way to Windsor via the Blue line. She wanted to help. Time was running out and Lupo needed all his friends if they were going to get to the bottom of what Vulcan was up to and find the evidence they needed for the trial.

Now she was waiting at the bottom of the kitchen staircase at Windsor Castle. A footman who had been serving the royal family their pre-dinner cocktails in the drawing room, nearly tripped over her. He bent down, looking for a collar. Grateful for

155

the attention she licked his big pink hand with her sandpaper-like tongue.

"Where did you come from?" he said. "I don't think I have ever seen a cat in the castle before . . ." he said as she sauntered off to investigate.

A rich aroma of fish filled the air.

"Scottish salmon – delicious!" She curled her long tongue around a sharp tooth.

The kitchen was busy. Carefully, Kitty bent her lithe body past several chefs, weaving in and out of their strong legs. Hoping for a taste, she didn't have to wait long before a plate of fresh fish landed smack on to the floor.

"DON'T DROP THE FISH!" yelled a large round woman.

"Yes, Chef," replied a young lad.

"WE GET ONE SHOT AT THIS BANQUET! I WANT ALL OF YOU ON YOUR FINEST FORM," yelled the Chef. "FIRST COURSE LEAVES IN TWENTY MINUTES."

Kitty settled herself into a corner and watched, waiting for an opportunity. The journey from Kensington had been a long one and she was hungry. Once fed she could go and find Lupo. Between her paws she toyed with a little charm for his collar – she had been saving it for his birthday.

St George's Hall had never been so busy. Lupo watched as servants filled the room. They moved like a well-oiled machine. One team carefully measured knives and fork positions along the longest table he had ever seen. Another team was polishing glasses and setting out gold plates, and a final team was standing on the table with bagged feet! They delicately walked along the table between the place settings, arranging candelabra and flowers.

"I think the plan should work. Everyone ready?" Herbert asked Lupo.

"Yes, but I think it's risky."

"Look, we need a distraction. We can't get to the room with the clock without tripping the castle's alarms. Whoever is playing that clock will be there tonight and they will be using the banquet as an excuse to play the clock. We need to catch them in the act."

"I agree with Herbert," said Holly. "Lupo, isn't there another way? The whole family will be here and I don't think the Queen will be happy."

Lupo knew his plan was risky but he wanted to catch Cyrus's attacker red handed. "Holly, I promise this will work! Everyone into position and good luck!"

It was the first chance they had been given to get into the state apartments. Lupo and Holly managed to squeeze past two page boys who were busy putting the finishing touches to the long table.

It was a magnificent sight. Each guest had six perfect crystal glasses, with every piece of cutlery polished to perfection. It would be a beautiful state banquet. The Ambassadors to India, Germany and Italy were all invited, together with members of parliament and all of the royal family. Tonight meant a great deal to everyone. The Duke and Duchess were especially looking forward to it since it was rare they got to attend formal banquets since Prince George's birth.

Right on the dot of eight o'clock the guests made their way through the Great Hall to their places for dinner. At 8.15 pm the royal family arrived and were seated. Then at 8.20 pm, Her Majesty the Queen walked into the hall. The entire table stood for the national anthem and it was around about then that, behind every doorway, Lupo's army assembled.

Organizing a thousand mice at short notice was not as hard as Herbert had originally thought. The mice felt duty-bound to assist Lupo who had shown them nothing but kindness since his arrival with the Duke and Duchess. It was the general opinion of the mice community that Lupo was in fact innocent. Only a small handful of mice thought otherwise.

The call had gone out earlier that afternoon and, just before the dinner began, the army of mice made their way to their positions. Behind every door leading to St George's Hall, there were over a 150 mice. All of them were waiting for their moment. As the final bars of *God Save the Queen* rang out, the mice made ready and somewhere under the long table Holly and Lupo waited, ready to run.

"Good evening," said the Captain of the Queen's Guard, standing to attention, ready to present the Queen.

That was the signal.

A thousand mice charged towards the middle of the dining room. The first wave clambered all over

the chairs, gripping on to the guests and then diving head first on to the table.

The hall was filled with terrifying screams. The VIP guests had never seen anything like it. St George's Hall was over-run by mice!

Alarms rang all over the castle.

Lupo and Holly ran – they ran as fast as their paws could carry them.

"Holly, run! There's no time to gander. The guards will be running into that hall any second. We won't have long to get to the clock before they stop the alarms!"

They raced past a neatly-presented bedroom and then a robing room.

"It's around the next corner," mewed Holly, having trouble keeping up with Lupo's long strides.

As they approached, however, they heard voices coming from the room, and stopped in their tracks. Looking around an open doorway, they saw two men wearing long green conservation aprons and white gloves, standing alongside the organ clock.

"Fred and Marvin," whispered Holly. "They're the Keepers of the Clocks. I don't understand what they are doing here now!"

Fred was in his early sixties, slim and pale and balding; Marvin was slightly younger and stocky, and he boasted a beard and a thick thatch of hair.

"Those alarms, I don't know why they have us fixing this clock when they really should be more concerned with those alarms," said Marvin. "That's the third time this month they have gone off!"

The alarms stopped.

"Good – someone pushed the button. I feel half deaf, Marv."

"Bloomin' loud, Fred."

"It baffles me, Marv . . . I can't see nothing wrong with the clock. It must have been some kids. It's always kids. They get those tiny ickle fingers of theirs and jam them into everything. They think this clock is a toy. They should take it off the tour, I tell you, they should, Marv."

"All I know, Fred, is that the guards have sworn that they have heard it *binging* away all on its own for weeks now and they are fed up with having to send someone up here to check it out. I told them that it was impossible – this old thing hasn't worked for years!"

Scratching his sweaty, bald head, Fred approached the clock. "Better get it down to the workshop and have it checked out. Public are back after the weekend and there will be hell to pay if it's not on show come Monday morning."

Marvin looked miserable. "And to think I could be sitting at home with my feet up. Can you hear that, Fred?"

"It's screaming, Marv – coming from the Hall!"

"Here, we'd better get out of here – sounds like trouble . . . better hurry. Here, you get General Gordon's bible."

Lupo and Holly were hiding behind a sofa. They watched as the two men carefully removed a solid gold statue from the top of a glass case.

The case was finely decorated, with a lace cushion inside it. Lying open for the world to see was the Gordon bible, Queen Victoria's most treasured gift.

"Easy now, Marv, don't want to drop it, do we?"

"This glass case, it's heavy!" complained hairy big Marvin, gripping the edge of the case.

"Wait! Not like that, Marv," shouted the thin, weak-looking Fred.

And that was it. The bottom dropped off the case, and the bible fell off its pillow and onto the floor.

"Look what you've done, Marv! Quick! Let's get

this heavy case onto the loading trolley. We'll have to come back for the bible."

Holly and Lupo waited until the two were safely out of earshot.

"Something fell out of the bible, Holly, did you see it?"

Carefully sniffing around the bible, Lupo found a folded-up piece of paper. It smelt of dust, age and, oddly, like burnt toast.

"There isn't much time, Lupo . . . What is it?" said Holly.

Lupo unfolded the paper. "It's a map."

Fred and Marvin were on their way back. There was no time to check out the rest of the organ clock. Another clock in the King's dressing room next door struck seven just as a hundred or so mice ran through the state rooms, carrying as much food as they could take from the state banquet.

The alarms sounded again and Lupo and Holly knew that was their signal to leave. "At least," thought Lupo, clutching on to the map from the bible, "we're not leaving empty-handed."

12
Kitty's Gift

The last of the mice had been caught by a group of weary-looking castle servants. It had been a long night. Kitty watched as the tired staffers returned to the kitchens. From their conversations she heard that the state banquet had been a disaster – something about mice.

As the last of the miserable chefs left the kitchen, she jumped on to a worktop on which someone had left what remained of dessert. Inside it there were three mice. They were singing to each other whilst sinking merrily in and out of the creamed sugar.

"This has been the best banquet EVVVVEEERRR!" one said.

"SUGAR!" yelled another.

"I'M SWIMMING IN A POOL OF DELIGHT!"

165

shouted the third.

Kitty was tempted to eat all of them. It had been ages since she had got her paws on a nice big juicy mouse. She was unable to eat the mice at Kensington Palace – limited only to chasing them because they all seemed to be cousins of Herbert's, or worse, they were part of M.I.5. It was a pitiful thing to be reduced to stalking but never actually getting her teeth into one . . . or . . . two . . . possibly even three. Looking around her, she fought the urge. "Too easy," she thought.

Now that all the humans had left the kitchen, it seemed to come to life with mice everywhere. From her perch on top of the butcher's block, Kitty watched as they skated on slippery tiles covered in cooking fat, oil and butter. She licked her lips as they cleaned up bits of cooked food fallen from dirty pans.

A group she was eyeing up suddenly scattered like marbles when a large, dirty-looking, old black buck rat appeared.

Kitty stared at the rodent, like a lion about to pounce on its prey. The more she studied it, however, the more it revolted her, and, after thirty seconds or so, she lost interest. She didn't even bother to follow the overly-ripe specimen as it staggered towards the larder in search of leftovers.

There was something strange about it. It was brazen. She had never seen a rat in the palace. They never dared. The more she watched it, the more curious she became. It walked as if it had a right to be in the kitchen, almost like it had been given permission.

Her eyes narrowed. From the top of the kitchen counter she waited and, as it left the room, she followed it through the Palace. It was up to something. She followed it all the way to a storm drain near the chapel. It squeezed through an iron grate and disappeared. Hiding behind a red postbox, she watched as it reappeared twenty minutes later. The rat was acting really suspiciously. It appeared to be shouting to something in the drain.

"Yes, sir, I'll give you the signal when it's done. Vulcan won't see us coming," it said.

Kitty watched as it bounded off back into the castle. She had to find Lupo.

The trick was to follow the baby's cries. Lupo liked to sleep near Prince George.

She found him asleep near a pop-up cot. The Duchess was asleep in a chair next to Prince George, who was awake, burbling loudly.

Lupo didn't stir as she carefully removed a bit of paper from between his paws. Absent-mindedly, she put the smart charm on the floor next to him. Distracted by the paper, she began to unfold it.

"A map," she purred.

The map, old and creased, was hard to read, but Kitty felt sure she had seen it before. She ran down to the tourist entrance and compared it with the map on the wall. Sure enough, they were of the same place: Windsor Castle. The main clue was the large octagonal courtyard in the middle.

"Upper Ward . . . that must be that, and what's this?" she said to herself. It looked like an X, but it could have been a date. She was unsure. Convinced she could help, however, she decided not to go back and wake him but, instead, to see where the map led.

Twenty minutes later, after a few false starts, she came to a smart red and gold room. That was when she managed to trigger the silent alarm. The map's X was a painting of Henry VII's family with St George and a rather angry-looking snakelike dragon.

Kitty was not in the least bit prepared for what happened next.

Music disturbed her. She looked for the source of the funny song. Her tail bashed against something hard. Turning back to the painting, she felt something move.

Then a "CLICK".

The next thing she felt was heat, and something grabbing her, and, as the map fell to the floor, she began to scream.

Kitty's screams were heard all over the castle. Lupo woke with a start. His ears pricked up. Something awful was happening.

By the time the guards had burst into the private apartments, Lupo was gone. Running through the castle, looking in every room, he searched frantically for the source of the screams. A chill ran the length of his soft, black coat. He knew something terrible was happening deep within the castle walls. Only when he came to the incredible painting did he stop. He smelt burning and rotten eggs.

Sniffing the ground and walls and skirting boards, he caught the whiff of something else as well: cat.

Kitty's unmistakable scent was *everywhere*. And then, inspecting the area closest to the painting, he discovered something more worrying still: blood, scratches and a scorched floorboard.

Madly, he began scratching the floorboard. "KITTY," he called out, listening for her but not hearing a sound except for the alarms.

A castle guard caught a hold of him and returned him to the Duke and Duchess's rooms. He was in serious trouble now. The guards shook their fists, blaming him for causing the noise that had disturbed the whole castle. The Queen would hear about it in the morning.

George waited until everyone had gone and *goo-ed*. "Lupo, are they going to take you away?"

Lupo couldn't answer his friend.

George sat down at the end of his cot with a humpf. "I wish I was bigger."

Lupo showed his white teeth in a smile, and then licked George's button nose. "Me too. Me too. We'd better get some rest. I have a feeling tomorrow is going to be a really long day."

The rest of the servants went back to bed bewildered and confused. The Duke and Duchess reluctantly agreed that this was the final straw – Lupo's fate was set.

Afraid that Lupo may cause another incident, the guard insisted on tying him to a table leg in the nursery, since he was refusing to leave Prince George.

The Duke said to the Duchess, "He's guarding George. I think we had better let him stay here for the night."

The Duchess agreed.

Lupo struggled, trying to get away from the lead. It was no good. He needed to rescue Kitty from whatever lurked behind the painting. He was stuck. He felt like he had put everyone in danger. He blamed himself.

All he could do was try and get some sleep and wait until morning. He needed Herbert and Holly. They were the only hope he had of getting free of his bonds. His paws smelt bad. "Rotten eggs," he thought, "better not mean what I think it does."

Just as he was closing his eyes, he noticed the charm that Kitty had left for him on the floor. Stretching on the lead, he managed to reach it with his front paw. *LUPO HRH* was scratched on to the front of it. It was the nicest present he had ever been given. Tied around it was a note that read:

To Lupo,

Thanks for being the best friend a cat could have.

Kitty

* * *

Herbert and Holly were both standing in Lupo's view first thing the next morning. He sat up, feeling the leash around his neck.

"Someone has Kitty," he declared, picking up the charm. "I found this by my bed last night." He showed them the charm. "The map was gone. She must have come in late last night and taken it."

"Well, my team are on the case – blood and hair samples were taken from the scene," said Herbert. "There was also a burnt floorboard – and a very strange smell."

"Yes, I know. I caught that, too – mingled with the unmistakable smell of mog. As much as I could smell her, though, I couldn't find her. Before the guards brought me here."

"What does it all mean?" asked Holly. "Why would anyone want to take Kitty? It makes no sense."

"I can only think that she was trying to help solve the mystery on her own," said Lupo. "Herbert, do you or any of your team have any ideas what the damage and the smell are all about? Could the scorched floorboard be from the great fire some years ago?" Lupo felt desperate – he was worried for his friend's safety.

"No, no, no, that board was burnt by something last night," said Herbert. "The heat was still on it when magpie and mice forensics arrived. Kitty could have been carrying a candle – but that seems unlikely."

Standing to his full height, Lupo tried and failed to swallow his frustration. "We have to find her before it's too late."

13
St George's Ring

The ring had been the key to unlocking the secret. There were no instructions about how to use it with the organ clock, though Vulcan had struggled to work out that it had to be placed on to a serpent's head located on the edge of the clock itself. Once the ring was on it, the organ opened.

Night after night, Vulcan had crept out of the Queen's bedroom to try out the numbers on the organ and . . . nothing. Then, just as he was about to give up, it worked. The musical instrument had not been wound correctly for decades, but, as the broken melody began, a secret entrance revealed itself behind the painting of St George, the dragon and King Henry VII's family.

The cave revealed more than he could ever have imagined. The Norman King, William the Conqueror, must have been in such a rush to hide the dragon that he'd forgotten to clear the cave of tons and tons of the finest English treasure.

Gold, jewels, helmets, swords and goblets littered the floor. It was spread out in great piles on tables, as if on sale at a school fair.

Vulcan sniffed the intoxicating scent of the power he had long desired. The dragon itself was asleep on a pile of golden coins in the middle of the darkest part of the cave. It smelt him and quickly flew to attack but was stopped in its tracks by the mere sight of the ring Vulcan twirled nervously around his paw.

Vulcan felt like he could change the world.

After the disaster that was the banquet, Vulcan had made his way to the Queen's bedroom. Her Majesty was too distracted to notice him leaving with the ring and the sword.

He was just finishing sliding the ring on to the serpent's head to begin playing the clock when he saw the Kensington Palace tabby entering the room, clutching what looked like a treasure map. "I can't

risk her spoiling my plan," Vulcan mumbled to himself as he began to play the dragon's melody.

The dragon was restless, hungry and fed up with being led up and down the tight exit route. Vulcan had prepared it well for tonight. But as the painting clicked open, it had lunged and grabbed the fearful cat, her screams ringing in Vulcan's long, pointy ears.

"TAKE HER DOWN TO THE LAIR AND STOP HER FROM SCREAMING – SHE'LL WAKE THE ENTIRE CASTLE," he ordered.

The dragon was enormous – far bigger than the tight entrance to the castle. Vulcan held his breath, shocked at the size of it. The rounded black scales on its belly shimmered in the moonlight.

Concerned that it might turn on him, Vulcan kept the heel of the sword in his hand. The Ascalon Sword was his only protection – the dragon feared it. All he had to do if he felt it was coming too close was grab the handle of the short but terribly sharp blade and point it. The threat was enough to stop the dragon in its tracks.

With its long talons wrapped around the cat, it watched Vulcan grumbling louder. The walls shook. An explosion of fire ripped through the red and gold room as a long black tail flicked with pent-up frustration. Another flaming ball shot from its black mouth, revealing a set of sharp teeth.

"STOP THROWING YOUR FIRE BALLS AROUND – OR ELSE I WILL USE THIS SWORD! SO HELP ME I WILL BRING YOU DOWN, BEAST," Vulcan said.

The dragon retreated, bending itself back into the cave and retreating into its golden bed. Vulcan followed, watching as Kitty struggled helplessly in its mighty grip. She had put up an impressive fight. The whole castle had been woken by her battle with the beast.

Vulcan watched her as she staggered towards a small stream that ran through the cave.

"You won't get away with this, Vulcan. We're all on to you," Kitty said. She was terrified of the dragon. But the dragon had its gaze fixed on Vulcan now, digging its talons into its gold. Kitty hoped the dragon would attack Vulcan, but she was disappointed. Instead it recoiled from the royal dorgi at the mere sight of the Ascalon Sword.

"MY DRAGON!" Vulcan was bold. He walked straight up to the mouth of the dragon and carefully stroked the side of its face, careful to ensure that it could see the sword. He turned to face Kitty, daring to turn his back on the dangerous dragon. Menacingly, he twisted the ring under his thick fur round and round.

The dragon appeared to respect its meaning and stood perfectly still, waiting to be told what to do. The fireball it had been saving now broke to the surface in a very loud roar. Too weak to scream, too weak to move, Kitty flattened herself limply to the floor of gold.

Vulcan laughed as she cowered. "Oh yes I will. I don't have time for you, *cat*. Thanks to you, I have had to change my plans. You *will* stay here until I return. Any attempt to escape and my friend here will enjoy destroying you."

Kitty screamed again, hoping that someone would hear her.

"No one can hear you; this cave is deep in the mound." Stepping away, Vulcan stopped and looked down at Kitty's tiny tabby body, shaking in horror. "Here's an interesting fact for you to think about whilst you are dying. We are actually in the middle of the Upper Ward of the castle . . . Funny how no one ever worked it out before me! I found the secret and so it belongs to ME! You will obey ME! If you try ANYTHING I will have MY dragon destroy you. I AM THE TRUE MASTER. I AM THE NEW KING OF ENGLAND!"

"Lupo will get you, Vulcan – of that I am sure," she replied confidently.

"LUPO? I don't think so. No – he will be gone by tomorrow morning. There is no chance of him coming to get you . . . No one will come and rescue you. Goodnight, cat!"

Kitty watched Vulcan disappear up a flight of stone steps, and then she was alone with the dragon. Its huge eyes seemed to be assessing her. Carefully she sat as still as she could, praying that Lupo had heard her cries and that Vulcan was wrong.

Lupo was her only hope.

One bite and she would be gone.

The Queen would be missing Vulcan. Over the years, he had worked out that he could be gone for long periods of time – but as long as he was back for Her Majesty's morning walk she didn't mind. Inside the dark cave, however, he had no way of knowing what time it was. He had to hurry back.

As he followed the steps out he could hear that the alarms were still ringing. This was good. It meant that he could return without having to avoid tripping all the laser alarms.

The beast would enjoy munching through Kitty's thin cat bones. She had looked so weak and pathetic. Pleased with his handiwork, Vulcan clicked shut the entrance. His rough coat ruffled, which gave him enormous pleasure. Twisting the ring, he felt invincible.

14
A Change of Plan

Claw had been watching events unfold from behind a pillar inside the heart of the cave. Carefully, he followed the power-crazed dorgi out to the quadrangle. He slipped back between the iron grate of the storm drain. Edgar, the famous Tower of London raven, was waiting for him, and he never liked to be kept waiting. Claw had to hurry.

The buck rat had been surprised to discover the secret dragon at Windsor Castle. Hidden in the shadows, he had watched as the cat was taken. Thankfully, the dorgi and the dragon had been too interested in the cat to notice him sneaking in and studying every aspect of the cave and its magnificent contents. Edgar would be pleased with him. He had worked hard lying to Vulcan – making him believe that he was the one in charge. Ha! He and Family Claw would get a nice reward, which would come in handy. Struggling under the weight of his miserable gut, he came to the large sewage tunnel and dived in.

Edgar was in a bad mood. He resented having to wait for Claw. When Claw appeared, the smelly fat rat said, "Your report, sir. Vulcan is planning something big."

"Well – what has he been up to?" Edgar replied. "You know I don't like leaving the Tower. Ravens don't belong in sewage tunnels. You had better have a good reason for getting me here, Claw. Your reports on Vulcan have been weak to say the least. The royal dog doesn't seem like much of a threat. What exactly *is* he up to?"

"It's a dragon, sir."

"A what?" Edgar asked slowly.

At the top of his voice, Claw spoke. "A DRAGON, SIR. Vulcan has found a dragon in the castle. An old one. Been there for a while. Wasn't sure at first what he needed the ring for but . . ."

Edgar stopped moving. He turned back to face the loyal rat. "Impossible – A DRAGON?"

"YES."

"Why are you shouting at me, Claw?"

"Because you are shouting at me."

"Don't."

"Yes, sir."

"Where did he get the dragon from?"

Claw told Edgar all about Windsor Castle's secret cave. The bird hopped furiously around. Until finally, when the rat came to the bit about the bed of gold, he exploded, "GET ME THAT RING, CLAW!"

"Why do you want it, sir?"

"Stupid question, Claw! I want to control that dragon. Vulcan has no idea what forces he's playing with. England will fall if the dragon is freed. Nothing will survive; there will be no Animal Kingdom, no human slaves! There will only be scorched earth. It's an ancient law: no ground dweller can control the might of the sky! HE MUST BE STOPPED. HE HAS GONE TOO FAR." Edgar flapped his thin wings in annoyance. Then he furiously kicked a half-eaten Tower of London toffee at the rat.

Claw was lost and confused. It was far less a reward than he'd been expecting.

15
The Saints Go Marching In

Nanny had eventually untied Lupo. It was unclear whether she did it because she felt sorry for him or because she wanted him out of the nursery. Either way, he wasn't waiting around for the guards to remove him.

There was no time to waste. Kitty was out there, alone and probably in great danger. Tying her gift on to his collar, he swore he would get her back to safety. Herbert had promised to look back in the archives for a copy of the map Kitty had taken. Holly had gone back to the Queen's chambers to keep an eye on Vulcan.

Lupo knew that it was a bad idea to head back to the clock but he had smelt Kitty there the night before and knew that it might be his last chance before the Queen had him removed from the castle for being a troublemaker. As he walked through the grand old castle, the mystery unravelled in his mind.

"The story had to be true. If St George really did exist, then why not a dragon?" he asked himself. "The burnt floorboard, the smell of rotten eggs . . . Deep in this castle there's a dragon – that's what all this is about. Windsor has a secret dragon! The organ clock had to be the key to finding it. Kitty was snatched right by the picture – that had to be the entrance to its cave; it had to be a hidden doorway. The only thing left to figure out was who attacked Cyrus."

Lupo felt no elation. He stopped, realizing that there was no way for him to get around the alarm. It was as he was standing there, in the middle of the hall, that a young mouse began pulling on his left paw. There was something vaguely familiar about it.

"My name is Tilly and you are Lupo," the little thing said, wide-eyed.

Lupo rarely spoke to the younger mice in Kensington Palace. When he was a puppy he had tried but the problem was that they were all so shy. Not Tilly, though. "Have we met before, Tilly?" Lupo said.

"Yes," said Tilly. "I saw you in the chapel. My mummy thinks you are guilty. But I don't think you did all the bad things everyone says you did."

"Thanks, Tilly," said Lupo. "I need all the help I can get at the moment." Without realizing it, he started to wag his tail. His thoughts then turned back to finding Kitty. Every minute that passed was a minute too long. Kitty was a big part of his family and he had to rescue her.

Tilly was busy climbing up his front leg now. "Are you looking for something?" she asked.

"I'm looking for—" Lupo took a moment, worried that he might scare his tiny new friend, who was now clinging on to his collar "—a very big, old animal. Hidden somewhere in the castle."

"Like Daisy? She's really old . . . even older than . . ." Tilly was distracted by the size of his ear, so she lifted it up to inspect what was inside.

"Who is Daisy, Tilly?" Lupo's ear was tickling. He resisted the urge to scratch it.

"Daisy the dragon! She's my friend. Doesn't like being stuck under the castle much. I think she's lonely. Wow you have big ears!!"

Lupo stood, routed to the spot, "DAISY?" he said it out loud. It seemed like a strange name for what was supposed to be a terrifying beast. "Tilly, can you help me—"

The little mouse fell out of his ear and swung haphazardly on the end of his earlobe. "YOU WANT ME TO HELP YOU? Oh this is the best day ever! Wait till I tell my friends – Lupo the royal dog and me!" the mouse replied excitedly, thrilled at the prospect of an adventure.

"Only, if you have the time?" But he needed her help. There was no way he could get to Kitty or Daisy the dragon without tripping the alarms again.

The mouse was over-excited, "I do, I do, I do," she sang out.

"Good. Right, firstly I need you to take me to the royal dog, Vulcan . . ."

The small mouse interrupted him and looked sad. "Oh," she said.

"What's wrong, Tilly?" he asked. As she swung madly from his earlobe he couldn't help but notice how frightened she seemed.

"Vulcan is horrible!" she whispered loudly.

"He's a mean royal dog . . . no one likes him. Mum makes us hide whenever she sees him. I think he has done some very bad things . . ."

Lupo didn't want to begin to thinking about all the other awful things the pompous royal mutt was capable of. "It's OK, Tilly. I know Vulcan is a bad dog. I just need to find Holly. She's not bad, is she? Do you think you could help me find her?"

"Holly is nice. Sometimes she reads to us. I like Holly. All the mice like Holly. I saw her not so long ago – she was heading towards the kitchen. Mum's going to kill me – I was meant to be there half an hour ago, but my shoes are too big and I keep tripping over in them." The tiny thing pointed to some undone black shoes that did indeed look far too big. "CARRY ME!" she begged. "You can carry me to the kitchen. That's where they'll be!"

Lupo ran all the way, with the mouse whooping with delight. When they arrived, Holly was staring at the castle map. "Holly, we have to hurry. I have figured it all out."

"And there was I thinking you would be stuck to a leash. Should have known you'd get free! Is that Tilly on your back?"

Tilly was laughing. Her head was jiggling from side to side.

Lupo lifted his paw up to give Tilly a chance to get down safely. Holly looked on disapprovingly.

"I know where Kitty is," he said, ignoring Holly's look of disapproval.

The little mouse, giddy with happiness, hopped on to his black paw. "MUM!" she shouted, seeing a gang of concerned mice gathering around the royal dogs.

Tilly's mother rushed forwards, happy to see her 601st baby safe. "Thank you for getting her back to me, Lupo. I thought she may have been caught up in one of those new traps they have laid since the banquet last night."

Lupo bent low, his nose nudging Tilly affectionately. "Any time you need a ride, Tilly, you just ask. Thanks for all your help. I promise you, I will stop Vulcan and I will help Daisy." The kindly mother mouse seemed proud of her youngest child's latest friendship.

As Lupo and Holly headed out of the kitchen, Holly asked, "Who's Daisy?"

"A very lonely old dragon," replied Lupo, a

lopsided smile spreading across his face.

"What did you just say?"

"There's a dragon, right here in the heart of Windsor Castle, and it's got Kitty."

Holly was shocked. "That's not possible. There is no such thing. Dragons are myths."

"A few weeks ago I would have said the same thing," said Lupo. "Holly, you are just going to have to trust me. I'm pretty sure I have figured out what's going on here – well, most of it."

Holly was in a state of shock. "I take it you mean a mechanical or animatronic dragon? We talked about this and you said that a real one couldn't possibly exist – it would be hundreds of years old!"

"Well, if Herbert says that there is a super crocodile in the Thames why wouldn't there be a dragon hiding in the Queen's castle?" replied Lupo, grabbing Holly's paw.

The two dogs raced to the entrance to the state rooms. Fred and Marv were carrying the clock back to its plinth. The two dogs followed quietly behind them. When Fred had finished sliding it into place, Marv suggested they go get a nice cup of tea.

Lupo was relieved that it was on display again and felt strongly that playing with it was the key to getting Kitty back. It glinted and gleamed in the winter sunshine. On top of the smart old clock was a golden statue of St George, fighting an evil dragon with a snake wrapped around it. Lupo stood on his hind legs and reached up to look at it more closely.

"What are you doing?" Holly kept guard nervously, not wanting anyone to see them pawing the priceless antique.

"That's it, Holly! Don't you see?"

"It's a statue of a dragon, not an actual dragon . . . You're nuts!"

"Yes, well, my dear," said Herbert, who'd appeared from a hole in the skirting board. "Couldn't agree more, but you know what they say, don't you? Just because you're nuts it doesn't mean that you won't have a good idea, once in a while – law of probability and all that . . . Now, I've been looking for you both. I've just been rummaging through the Royal Archives – as you do – and I have some news. Within the animal section I found that a medieval music book had been signed out by Vulcan and has yet to be returned. But I found a copy of it on the internet."

Holly couldn't help but ask, "Herbert, are you telling me M.I.5 has figured out a way to use a human computer?"

"I've got fourteen of our fittest mice keyboard jumping. They seem to have a problem with the spacebar though . . ." replied Herbert, wriggling into the lock underneath the clock.

A strange ancient keyboard popped out. On it there were what appeared to be piano keys running from a deep low C to a light soft B.

"But . . . how?" asked Lupo.

Holly replied on Herbert's behalf. "Let me guess, the internet?"

Lupo studied the keyboard and then began to play the notes he had seen on the map.

Herbert corrected Lupo when he hit a bum note. Seeing the confusion on Holly's face he said, "On his deathbed, General Gordon left Queen Victoria a bible he'd carried hidden in his tunic. Inside it was the map you found. It gave the exact location of the dragon and how to access it in the event the ring was lost. One of my team found it yesterday. It must have drifted under the bottom of the curtains when Kitty was attacked."

Holly grabbed the map from Herbert's hand and ran behind the clock. "Lupo, it's that note – that is a C not a D!" Together the three of them watched as Lupo carefully finished putting in the notes.

"Here we go, Holly, I give you the dragon's song," said Lupo proudly.

As the strange music filled the room, Herbert's ear's twitched. "Hardly One Direction, is it!"

Holly listened, realizing what was about to happen but it was too late – there was no going back. "LUPO! It is too dangerous! STOP IT!"

Ancient music poured from the organ clock. All the animals looked at each other in amazement. As the music reached a crescendo and filled the room, the painting once again clicked open.

Holly was speechless. Rooted to the spot, she couldn't budge. Herbert had no such reservations and marched straight up to a stone entrance. Looking around the edge of the doorway, he noticed exactly what he had suspected. "It's all scorched," he announced, "there can be no doubt these are the markings of the dragon."

Lupo sniffed the air. "ROTTEN EGGS."

Holly spoke very slowly, but very firmly. "Lupo, do you have any idea how dangerous it would be if there was a live dragon in there? Do you?"

"Put simply – it would be the discovery of the century. Or, rather, quite a few centuries," he replied, hoping that Kitty was still alive.

It was not what Holly wanted to hear. "How can you be so irresponsible? Both of you!" she barked. "And to think I helped you! You have opened a gateway that has been sealed for hundreds of years! This is treason!"

Herbert grabbed Lupo's paw, stopping him from rushing in.

They all stopped as they were interrupted by a distant, but definite, ROAR.

16
Enter the Beast

Standing in the middle of the entrance to the cave, Lupo and Herbert listened as the roar got louder and louder, thundering down the stone corridor.

"Lupo, if we go in, there's a strong chance we will not make it out!"

"I know, but Kitty . . . I *know* she is still alive."

Holly was furious and fearful all at the same time. "You are not going in there – it's not safe!"

"We have no idea what we are going to be up against, and we have no way of fighting it . . ." added Herbert.

"I'm going in," responded Lupo.

Herbert saw the determination on the cocker spaniel's face, "Think, dear boy, think. Just for a minute or two, *think*. We need a plan. We can't just burst in and hope she's waiting for us!"

"I have a plan. I'm going to go and get the guards and do this properly. So no one else gets hurt." Before either of them could stop her, she was running off down the hallway towards St George's Hall.

Herbert shook his head. "Er . . . that wasn't a good plan. If the humans discover this creature, worse things will happen. Dragons are rare."

"*Rare?* You mean there are others?" asked Lupo. "Daisy down there might not be the only one?"

Herbert did not reply. Instead, he pursed his little lips tightly shut.

"I'm going in," repeated Lupo.

Herbert shook his head and blocked Lupo from entering the cave. "Have you taken leave of your senses? We don't even know what type it . . ."

"Type?" he asked. He frowned in frustration and fear. Then, bracing himself, he took a deep breath. "Look, I'll give it my best shot. I'm fast, strong and I have to get Kitty, she's my friend."

Herbert sighed as deeply as Lupo breathed. "Roughly translated, that means that you are young, inexperienced and trouble just follows you around. Without me, you are done for. If you go in, I will have to go in, too."

"Herbert, it's Kitty . . . she's my family, please let me pass."

"OK, old chap, OK. *Contra dracones*."

"What?"

"Never mind. You first."

Lupo turned on his tail and walked into the darkness, the sound of his panting reverberating in the eerie stillness. Herbert was walking behind him. "Watch it, the ground isn't even . . . hang on a second . . ."

There was a loud whooshing sound. Herbert waited. Silence. "LUPO?" he asked bravely. Nothing. "Are you there?"

"I'm falling!" shouted Lupo.

"Me too!" Herbert shouted back.

They had both slipped off a steep ledge. Neither could see where they were or where they were heading. They fell, faster and faster. Branches scraped underneath them and at one point they were covered in water. The roar, which had faded, was now faint, but close. The beast had been disturbed by their screams as they tumbled to what they thought was certain death. With a crash and a bump, they landed on top of what felt a little like the surface of a children's playground – rough but springy.

"Herbert, you there?" asked Lupo.

"I'm here, but frankly I have no idea where *here* is . . . can you see anything?"

"No. But the smell . . ."

Herbert felt something warm on his back. "Oh, that's nice, a little more to the left. Mice really don't like the cold. Thanks for warming me up, you are a good friend."

"I'm not warming you up."

"You're not?"

"No."

A pair of yellow eyes opened next to them both. Herbert felt something moving underneath. It slowly dawned on him that they had landed on the nose of the dragon and that he was resting on the pad of one of its scales.

"RUN!" Herbert yelled at Lupo. *"RUN!"*

Still lying down, the dragon shot a burst of flames out of its mouth.

Flames smouldered on tree roots creeping along the top of the cavern, setting them on fire. An orange glow revealed the dragon in all its awesome fiery glory

– and the pebbles of gold beneath its vast belly. The dragon hadn't noticed the tiny mouse, now running over its head and down its back. Dragging itself from its bed, it was far too busy trying to find Lupo. The dog and the clumsy dragon were soon locked in an awkward dance.

Herbert made a break for it. Seeing a small opening in the cave, he dived off the back of the beast and found himself at the bottom of some stairs. He watched as the dragon stood towering over the small cocker spaniel. Lupo barked wildly at it, but he was tiny in comparison. It was covered in thick chainmail-like skin that glowed in the burning lights.

Quickly, Herbert studied the dragon: short legs, long talons and a very fine pair of long vein-ridden leathery wings. Undecided, he waited to see its tail. Only the tail would give its true identity away.

He did not have to wait long. Lupo was growling at it, baring his teeth and grabbing the pebbles of gold scattered beneath his paws. The dragon whipped its tail around the cave furiously. There was a sharp barb on the end of it that looked like it could slice anything clean in half.

When he saw the distinct yellow arrowhead

marking on the tip of the dragon's tail, Herbert knew they were done for. The dragon was renowned for its killing prowess. Only one man was known to have survived its wrath and that was St George himself.

The tail moved again, and the barb landed so fast and hard on the ground it sent the gold flying through the air.

Lupo ducked under the belly of the beast and found some shelter behind a column at the side of the cave. As the beast grew more and more frustrated, Lupo called out to Herbert. "Find Kitty and get her out of here!"

Herbert counted to five, built up as much courage as he could, and ran down the side of the cave.

Meanwhile, the mouth of the dragon attacked over and over again, trying to tear down the column standing between it and the dog. Its bloated belly pulsated.

Herbert ran and ran, searching every nook and cranny for Kitty. The cave was enormous. It was also very deep. They had to be in the very centre of the mound.

Tall columns rose out of the ground, holding up

ancient arches. The whole castle had to be resting on top of this super-structure. The vast space was also full of gold. Polished by the dragon's belly, it shone brightly in the fiery glow.

Herbert was about to give up when he heard something moving. He bounced over the worn gold. There, behind a large golden throne, was the tabby cat. She was lying on the floor.

"Kitty! You're alive! Thank Mother Nature!"

She was less enthusiastic. "Get me out of here. Mother Nature owes me a holiday!"

Herbert stumbled and tripped over skeleton bones of what appeared to be a cat. "Well, at least that solves the mysterious lack of cats in the royal households," he said. "They must all end up here. That's one case file I can finally close."

"So glad to have been of service! Where's Lupo?"

"He's distracting the dragon."

She drew in a large gulp of air. "He's signed his own death warrant, more like! HE NEEDS OUR HELP!"

Roaring filled the hall. Everything started to shake. Dust fell from the ceiling of the cave. The column Lupo was hiding behind crumbled into a pile, and the dragon lunged at him once again. All he could do was close his eyes and pray.

17
Daisy Unchained

The dragon opened its jaws widely – but closed them, empty.

Vulcan was back in the cave, twisting the ring and flashing the sword, controlling the dragon. "It appears I've arrived just in time to see the show!" he said, and the beast recoiled.

Lupo blinked, unsurprised to see Vulcan. He felt rage boiling inside him. The Queen's villainous dorgi had betrayed everyone. "You have no idea what you are doing, Vulcan. You have to stop," he said.

Vulcan laughed. "One day, you will understand that this is for the best. Every animal will thank me."

"Your pet dragon will destroy everything. There will be nothing left."

"Lupo, you are so innocent and . . . *stupid* . . . It

205

will soon be time for us to say goodbye."

Bewitched by Vulcan, the dragon shot flames all around the cavern. Lupo felt his tail being singed by the flames.

Herbert and Kitty watched Vulcan as he snared the dragon in some kind of trance. "Oh, Herbert, I don't like this – we had better think of something fast or else Lupo's had it," Kitty whispered.

Herbert closed his eyes and thought very hard. "The cry of the cat," he said at last. "The cry of the cat. Just might work. There might still be some kind of trigger in the dragon's brain."

"Herbert, stop rambling. What could be more dangerous than this? If you have some kind of plan, I want hear it – fast!"

"In ancient Egypt, cats, as I'm sure you know, had some kind of mystical significance – you know about the Sphinx. It was said that cats alone had the power to frighten demons and dragons."

"Really? A humble cat, tame a great big dragon?" Kitty replied, unsure of the little mouse's big plan.

"Yes, but we need the ring to stop it. At any minute Vulcan will need to twist the ring again around his grubby little paw – otherwise he may start to lose control." She watched as Vulcan fiddled with the little gold ring. "Of course Vulcan is winding that dragon up like a clockwork toy using the ring!"

"It appears so . . . We need to seize our chance . . . His power over the dragon is lapsing. I know you're weak, but, on the count of ten, I want you to scream as loud as you can. Give us your best, most painful cat call ever. Give us a shriek that could wake the dead!"

Herbert counted down from five, and Kitty did as she was told, screaming herself hoarse – and sure enough, before Vulcan had time to twist the ring, the dragon, hearing the awful cry, raced back down the corridor, tripping over gold as it fled.

Vulcan tried to follow it, but Kitty tripped him up with her tabby tail.

The dragon gone, Lupo emerged from behind the column.

Kitty had caught Vulcan's eye with her claw and disoriented him. As he struggled to get up, she rushed to Lupo's side. "I have never been so happy to see your black 'n' furry face!" she announced.

"Kitty, are you hurt?" Lupo scanned Kitty's thin frame for damages. She had a slight limp but other than exhaustion she seemed fine.

Kitty smirked. "I'll heal. Didn't you hear? Cats have nine lives. Even after this I've still got eight left!"

Lupo looked around for the exit.

"Hey, that puppy that showed up at Kensington Palace, the one that wouldn't stop following me around . . . yes I'm talking about you, Lupo . . . If I'd have known just how much of an adventure it was going to be living with you . . . well, I just may have to move! Don't ever drag me out of that laundry basket again!" Kitty mewed.

Lupo saw a staircase. "Get yourself to safety and find Holly, and, for heaven's sake, keep her out of here!"

Reluctantly Kitty agreed. Behind her were the narrow stone steps she hoped would lead back up to the castle. She limped her way up it, a mixture of relief and apprehension in her heart.

Alone, the cocker spaniel and the dorgi faced each other across the cave.

"Give me that ring, Vulcan. Give it to me before anything else happens," growled Lupo.

The dorgi twisted the ring and stood poised to attack the cocker spaniel if it came any closer. Lupo lowered his body to the ground and waited, crouched and ready to pounce.

"NEVER!" answered Vulcan. "THE DRAGON BELONGS TO ME! COME, MY BEAUTY; COME AND COLLECT YOUR PRIZE!"

Lupo heard once more the distant roar of the dragon. His whole back arched, he rammed himself into the side of the royal dorgi. Vulcan kicked back, viciously. On the golden floor of the cave, the dogs fought viciously, their teeth snarled and clashed, their paws ripped and scratched. As they rolled further and further into the gold, Lupo struggled to maintain his grip on the dorgi's collar – and Vulcan broke free.

"ENOUGH! It's high time someone taught you a lesson, princely pup!"

Swiping his paw across the cocker spaniel's nose, however, Vulcan left the ring exposed. Lupo turned his mouth to the dorgi's short but strong paw and caught the ring in his teeth. As the ring slipped on to his tongue, both dogs knew the fight was over.

The dragon re-appeared just as Lupo put the talisman on his front paw. Vulcan ran to the far corner of the cave and disappeared up a staircase.

Faced with the dragon, Lupo pointed his front paw at the beast. "Daisy, it's over . . ." he said, hoping the ring would keep him safe.

The dragon leaned forward and, with its huge nose, nudged Lupo. Looking around the cave, it seemed dazed and confused. "Where am I?" it said softly, in a strangely feminine voice.

"Daisy, my name is Lupo. You are in a cave in the middle of Windsor Castle, and boy, have I got a good story for you."

"Thank you for breaking the spell on the ring," said Daisy. "You must be a very fine and good-hearted knight."

Lupo looked fondly at the now gentle giant and smiled to himself. "I don't suppose you remember seeing a mouse in a rather tight green cardigan, do you?" he said.

Just then, there was a very faint shuffling sound. It was coming from an area of the floor where the gold had been dispersed. Herbert's ears were a little burnt from the dragon's breath, and his cardigan a little frayed, but, other than that, he emerged unscathed; even his glasses were intact.

Lupo looked in wonder at his friend and the beast, two extremes of the animal kingdom in one place.

"*Draco domesticus*," said Herbert. "Well, well."

18
The Knights' Table

Daisy, as it turned out, was not all that bad – though she did admit to eating a few of the villagers' cows, sheep and the odd cat. Herbert seemed a bit more relaxed in her presence now that Lupo wielded the Ring of St George. Lupo studied his new friend. "Daisy, we have to get you out of here. If they find you they will hurt everyone."

Daisy's heart lifted at the thought of freedom.

The burnt mouse stepped closer to Lupo. "If I may be so bold as to interrupt . . . There is still the matter of the missing Ascalon Sword. We need to find it. Whoever has it has the power to slay the dragon . . . sorry, I mean, Daisy."

"Yes, and that's not the only problem. Daisy, just how are we going to get you out of here?" Lupo said, looking around. "Herbert, I'm going to search for the sword. Vulcan must have stashed it somewhere close by. You two look for a way out."

"Er . . . all right," said Herbert. "Just make sure you twist that ring every half an hour or so, won't you?"

"There won't be any need for that," said Daisy. "Lupo is very much like my farm boy George. I like nice people and animals. Herbert, I can sense you know a lot about dragons but there is something you don't know. You see, we dragons know who has a wicked heart, and I only eat those who mean to harm me. Dragons are on the whole pretty pleasant creatures."

"Humble apologies, Daisy. It seems my library shall need some updating. Perhaps you can help fill me in . . ."

Lupo laughed as the mouse and dragon walked to the back of the cave. "Poor Daisy," he said to himself. "She'll never be free now!"

He headed straight into the gap in the wall and carefully made his way up a flight of stairs. At the top, was a landing and another staircase, which led back to the painting. Avoiding the staircase and turning left on the landing, he made his way along another passageway.

There were two things on his mind now: making sure Daisy was safe and bringing Vulcan to justice. Following the path, he came to a stone arch. Walking through it, he found himself in a big, round room. In its centre was a large heavy-looking wooden octagonal table. On the table were twenty-three swords, perfectly placed to point to the middle. They were the swords of the noblest of England's Knights – and it was clear one of them was missing.

Seconds later, he discovered why.

"WATCH OUT! BEHIND . . ." Kitty's voice boomed in his ear. Before he could turn to face her, he felt something hard strike his head, and he crumpled to the floor.

When Lupo came to, he was lying in the middle of the table, his paws all bound, with Kitty tied up next to him.

As they both wriggled to get free, Vulcan sat with the sword by his side on a solid gold throne. Clearly, the dorgi had intercepted Kitty as she attempted to escape from the caves.

"The dragon belongs to me," Vulcan sneered.

"Once the ring is back in my possession, I will control her – you'll see. All I need is the sword. She fears the sword above all other things. Its blade is sharp – St George's very own sword. Do you have any idea of the power I have?"

Lupo struggled against the ropes binding him and Kitty.

"From here, this will be my war room. Rather nice, isn't it? Who would have believed that it was hidden beneath Windsor all this time? Just think of the hundreds of thousands of people who have walked above, never for a second thinking that such a wondrous place was right beneath their feet. Humans, stupid creatures! I shall enjoy destroying them all. Once they are gone I will rule the world. Animals will be in charge. I shall be the true KING!"

"You're mad, Vulcan. If you think I will let that happen."

"Perhaps I will start with Prince George . . ." Vulcan knew exactly how to hurt Lupo. "Yes, seems only fitting that I should remove the heirs. Free the way for me."

Lupo barked loudly. He managed to free one of his paws. "Daisy!" But it was no good. She couldn't hear him.

"Now, if you will excuse me, I have to bring my dragon back under my control."

"Not so fast, Vulcan," came a voice at the doorway.

Lupo lifted his head to see a black raven blocking the doorway. Its beak looked worn and battered, its wings broken and beaten. Alongside it was a great big, black rat. Kitty knew it was the same ugly buck rat she had seen in the castle kitchen.

Vulcan pretended not to mind the intrusion. "Claw! How nice of you to join us. Who is our friend?"

The raven flew into the corgi's face. "I'm your worst nightmare!" he said, his beak pecking at the dorgi's paws.

"Vulcan, meet Edgar, my only master." Claw stood back, satisfied with his work.

Edgar's beady eyes studied Vulcan. "When Claw filled me in on your little scheme, I naturally had to pay you a visit. Claw, get the ring and give the signal to empty the cave."

Vulcan removed the ring from his paw and held it between his teeth, unwilling to give it to the rat who'd betrayed him.

"Don't try anything funny," said Edgar. "Swallow that ring and it might get caught on something inside you . . . Besides, Claw and his family would only follow you around until it passed out of you . . . Rats spreading disease through the royal homes – and your poo being the star attraction . . . My, my, my – what would Her Majesty think of that?"

Edgar smiled at the horrified look in Vulcan's eyes. Walking up to the pampered pooch, he snatched the ring out of Vulcan's mouth, and, with enormous pleasure, slowly slid the once powerful ring on to his ankle. The rat was about to get down from the chair when Edgar flicked his wings at a piece of old rope.

"NOT SO FAST!" he commanded. "Tie him up."

Using his teeth and his claws, the rat tied the corgi to the chair. Edgar rejoiced at the spectacle. "Go and see that they have not missed a single piece of my gold. I want that cave empty! *Empty*, do you hear me?"

Claw headed to the door to carry out the rest of his orders, bowing his head to his master as he left.

Edgar wasn't finished. "Right now, the entire rat colony is busy removing the dragon's gold. You will come to the Tower, so that I can work out what should be done with you."

Lupo lifted his head from the table. "Please, let me take care of Vulcan," he begged. "I will see that he comes before the Grand Jury."

"The Grand Jury? For what?" replied Edgar.

"For attacking Cyrus, the Imperial Swan."

The raven seemed suddenly unsettled. His head moved backwards and forwards and his eyes darted around the room. Then, recovering himself, he stilled his wings and stood proud and tall. "You have been misinformed. Claw was the one who stole the ring and the sword from the lake at Kensington Palace." Edgar strutted up to the captured dogs, his eyes full of menace.

Lupo, however, refused to be intimidated. "But at whose bidding, Edgar, whose bidding? You could hardly call Claw a criminal mastermind, could you?"

In the corner, Vulcan, moving from side to side, laughed. "It was all me, Lupo." Vulcan leaped down from the throne. While Edgar had been talking to Lupo, he'd managed to cut himself free using the sword. "Looks like the last laugh's mine."

Edgar puffed out his chest and let out a piercing whistle. In no time at all, three large rats appeared and jumped on the dorgi. The sword slipped from his paws and fell on to the table. Edgar was impressed by the rats' speed. "Nice work, boys, now GET HIM OUT OF HERE!"

The rats dragged Vulcan out of the room.

"The rats will be along shortly to close this room for ever," said Edgar to Lupo and Kitty. "How interesting they will find it hundreds of years in the future when they dig you both out. Cat and dog bones, buried together. How ironic. So long." He bowed before leaving the room.

Lupo and Kitty got to work, immediately trying to free themselves. It was no good. The ropes were too tight. They needed something sharp.

"Hang on!" Lupo dragged his body over to the side of the table.

They both said it together, "The Ascalon Sword!"

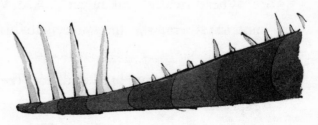

19
Edgar's Revenge

Rats swarmed all over the gold. Every piece was piled high on the backs of the worker rats. Claw stood guard, ensuring that nothing was missed. Edgar stood over Vulcan, his wings preventing the royal dorgi from trying to escape.

"Vulcan, Vulcan, Vulcan, it was all going so well, and then you had to get greedy and silly," said Edgar. He watched as the last pieces were removed. The remaining rats, stacked high with gold, staggered towards the dark corridor.

"Where are they taking it?" asked Vulcan, his voice unsure for the first time, and his weakness visible.

"I could lie to you, but I shall not. The gold is, as we speak, making its way under Windsor Great Park.

Ironically, it is the very same tunnel used to transport the dragon here all those years ago. Bit of a mess – Claw had to bring in every cousin, brother, aunt and sister. He had to clear it for today."

"So you knew about the gold all along?" asked Vulcan, shocked at having been outsmarted by the raven.

Edgar sighed heavily. "I have been around far too long, Vulcan. Many types have come – and gone – at the Tower. You are not the first of your kind, and you won't be the last. You were always going to need a lot of gold to take over the world. All I had to do was have Claw follow you – and lead me to the stash. You have, as I see it, two choices: remain hidden in the tunnels with the common rats or return to your old life with the Queen but agree to work for me." The raven paused. "Oh, silly me, I almost forgot. There's a third choice. The Grand Jury."

With the last breath of defiance left in him, Vulcan snarled, "And how exactly would that work, bird? You're just as tied up in that swan's murder as I am!"

Edgar cawed and threw back his head. "I think

you're forgetting something. Claw, if you would fill him in."

The rat stepped forward. "I could tell the Grand Jury that you told me to hurt the swan and frame Lupo."

At last, Vulcan was done. Outsmarted, he knew he was finished. "All right, all right. I'll return to the castle."

The raven snapped his beak. "And work as my slave?"

Vulcan replied through gritted teeth. "And work *with* you."

Full of wicked delight, Edgar cackled. "Run along now. I shall call on you when it's time. Oh, and bow to your master as you leave – don't show me your back. Walk out facing me, that's right. There's a good dog, a nice loyal subject."

Vulcan's thoughts turned to Daisy, who was slumped in the corner, controlled by the raven. "What about her?" he said, looking at the forlorn dragon.

"She will never be controlled by anyone again." Edgar hopped towards the dark corridor, leaned down to his foot and pecked off the ring. It broke in two. As it snapped, Vulcan whimpered.

Daisy charged towards the dog, the raven and the rat. All three of them took off, one flying deep into the darkness, and the other two running to keep up.

Returning from the round room, Lupo bounced in front of the dragon before it could catch any of them. "It's over, Daisy. Leave them to it."

Kitty looked around, "Look, all the gold . . . it's gone."

"I hate to think where. At least they've gone. Now all we have to do is get Daisy to safety."

Lupo was saddened. His plan to bring Cyrus's attacker to the Grand Jury had disappeared down a dark tunnel.

"How on earth are we're going to find our way out of here? I'm not sure Her Majesty is going be happy about a great big black dragon dragging its shiny wings through her castle," said Kitty.

"Well, that's just the beauty of it." Lupo smiled and winked at Daisy, who, at the other side of the cave, was walking into the dark corridor towards the tunnel under the park. "She gets to go back to wherever she came from. Safe travels, Daisy. I hope you find your way home."

Kitty was astonished. "Seriously? You're going to let a dragon roam freely home? What if it starts eating everyone?"

Lupo was still clutching the sword of St George. "I think Daisy has had enough of man," he said. "She knows we have the Ascalon Sword. I think that will be the last we see of her. We had better get back to the castle. Got to find some place to hide this thing."

"Yeah, like it's going be easy to hide a sword!"

"Actually, Kitty, I think I have just the place."

20
A Secret No More

Four dozen castle mice holding makeshift arms burst into the cave led by Herbert.

"Reinforcements!" cried the head of M.I.5, looking around. He was almost disappointed to find Daisy and Vulcan gone. "We missed all the action, did we?" he said.

Lupo and Kitty laughed. It was time to head back to the castle. One by one, the animals left the empty dark cave. Once they were all safely out, Herbert and the M.I.5 mice sealed the entrance.

Holly returned with two highly confused Queen's guards only to find Kitty looking battered, lying in front of the famous clock. They picked her up and took her back down to the kitchen to get a remedy for her burns and wounds – all she really wanted was to find a nice comfortable laundry basket.

Eventually, Lupo was left alone with the sword. It needed a good home. Apart from a bit of engraving, it looked much like any other sword, and that made it easier to hide. Lupo wandered through the fine state apartments to the throne room and armory and left it there. As he ambled out, he smiled wryly to himself. Everyone would be able to look upon the great knight's sword, and yet only he and his friends would know how special it was.

Lupo and Holly sat in the little living room in Windsor Castle – the Queen's most private space. Her Majesty had been informed that a strange injured cat had been responsible for the screams and not Lupo after all. Holly said that the Queen had told the Duke that she had a special affection for Lupo. It was their last night together before the Duke and Duchess headed back to Kensington Palace. Herbert appeared with good news.

"Cyrus is awake! He survived his surgery and is recovering nicely. Magpies visited him this morning. Marie Louise is over the moon to have her husband home. Just in time to see the new cygnets."

"That is fantastic, Herbert, how is his wing? Will he fly?" asked Lupo.

"It's possible," replied Herbert.

Holly was thrilled. "What about the attack? Has he said anything about Lupo?"

"Yes, yes, that is the best bit! Cyrus told the magpies and a rather annoyed-looking Percy that he was attacked by a big rat."

"Claw . . ." growled Lupo.

"Indeed, he said it was a buck rat. Described Claw – black fur, long tail, good swimmer." Herbert was shaking with glee.

"Does that mean it's over?" hoped Holly.

"Not quite, I have informed the authorities that it's Claw they need to be looking for. But I don't hold out much hope of them finding him. I suspect him and that raven will be long gone by now."

"With all that gold," added Holly.

"Claw's day will come," offered Lupo.

"Where *is* Kitty?" enquired Herbert.

"On her way back to Kensington Palace," Lupo answered. "She said she had some business to attend to."

Herbert excused himself. "Better dash, enormous amount of paperwork to do."

Holly looked at Lupo quizzically, "Do you think Kitty has gone after Claw?"

"I don't know. Last thing she said to me was that she wanted to check a few things out at the Tower of London," winked Lupo knowingly.

As the last of the young prince's baby things were packed into the boot of the car, Holly stood waiting to say goodbye. They had shared an amazing adventure, and both dogs were sad to be leaving each other.

"I'll see you soon," she said to Lupo, a tear rolling down her cheek. "Thank you for helping me."

Lupo leaned over and kissed the tear from the end of her nose.

Prince George was trying to watch the two dogs, as he was strapped into his car seat by the Duke.

"You had better get in or else you will miss your ride," said Holly, blushing. "Good luck."

"Bye," said Lupo, jumping into his bed in the boot of the car. "See you soon."

The journey home flew by. Lupo spent the entire journey telling George all about Vulcan's terrible plotting and the missing treasure.

"*Dats amoushy!*"(That's amazing!) George said

when at last the story was done.

As the car drove in through the large gates of Kensington Palace, Lupo looked up and saw Percy waiting for him. Once Lupo was freed from the boot, the imperious pigeon flew down from his post.

"I don't suppose you've heard the news, have you, hound? The Grand Jury has ruled. You're free. I've done you a disservice, dog – and I'm sorry I doubted you."

"That's OK!" Lupo replied. "Thanks, Percy. Hey, perhaps we can hang out sometime? Maybe you would like to join us on a walk tomorrow?"

Percy was delighted. "Well, yes, I'd love to."

"See you tomorrow, Percy," Lupo said running through the gates. He felt sure that nothing – not even the absence of Holly – could spoil this day.

"Stay out of trouble in future!" Percy called after him but somehow that seemed less likely.

Back in the nursery, the Duchess looked down at Lupo's tail. Nanny followed her gaze. "I was wondering if we ought to get that looked at," the Duchess said.

Nanny was confused. "Have you decided to keep him, then? What about all that trouble with the swan?"

"We've decided that he couldn't possibly have hurt that swan. We think he was trying to protect it from something. Funny how you just know your pets? Besides the Queen is quite taken with Lupo," replied the Duchess.

"Never doubted Lupo for a second," said Nanny. "He certainly does love Prince George. As for that tail, well – that lazy mutt does nothing but sleep – he must have caught it on a flame dozing by the fire. Silly cocker spaniel . . . Brain the size of a ping-pong ball."

The Duchess continued, "Nanny, whilst I have you here, the Duke and I were wondering if you wouldn't mind staying on another few years. We have some big news . . ."

Lupo made himself comfortable under the cot and smiled, happy to be home.

"Lupo, please can you tell me the story about the dragon again," said George after his mother and Nanny had left.

"Let me tell you about Daisy," Lupo growled.

"Yes! Yes!" screamed George, grabbing his toy

wombat and waving it in the air. "Roar!"

"Yes, George! It's Daisy the dragon."

The young Prince looked bewildered suddenly, "Daisy? Doesn't sound like a very scary dragon . . . does it?" interrupted the Prince.

"Let me tell you, Daisy is the scariest dragon of them all. She's vicious!"

"How vicious?" yelled George.

"Really nasty, George, and you know what – she's outside watching us right NOW!"

George was so delighted he screamed, because this was his favourite kind of bedtime story. "Roar Lupo, Roar!"

And with that, Lupo obeyed and roared as loudly as he could. "*Raaarrrrrrrgggghhhhh!*"

The Duchess listened to the noises coming from the nursery. She looked over at her husband who was watching the television and said, "If you ask me, all this roaring business started with that bedtime story of yours."

Epilogue

Claw scurried excitedly into Edgar's cell at the Tower
of London.

"How's it all going? Is it all safe and secreted
away?" asked Edgar.

"Not yet, sir. We found something in amongst it
all – and it sort of stopped us in our tracks."

"What is it?"

Claw removed an object from the pocket of his
work coat and rolled it towards his master.

"An egg, sir."

Here is a taste of Lupo's next adventure!

Lupo and the Curse at Buckingham Palace
is available from June 2015.

Prologue

Lupo glimpsed the picture on the front page of the Duke's newspaper. It was a black and white photograph of the Queen smiling in front of Buckingham Palace. Alongside her was a large telescope pointed up at the moon. It was nearly suppertime. Lupo's stomach groaned loudly, distracting him. He rolled on to his back, exposing a freckly pink underbelly so that Prince George could tickle him affectionately.

The Duchess was sitting on a smart red sofa in the

middle of the living room, putting the finishing touches to a letter she was writing on Kensington Palace paper. Sealing the envelope, she said, "The Queen's Birthday and the eclipse will be a special day tomorrow. So I think early bed for everyone, especially since Daddy is on night feeding duty tonight!" She walked over to her husband, the Duke, who carefully handed her the new baby. Prince George was a toddler and Lupo loved playing with him. They both looked forward to the day when they could play with the baby that seemed to have the whole world whipped up in a frenzy of love and excitement.

As the Duchess took the baby from her husband's arms, she looked down at the newspaper next to him. "What are you reading, darling?" she asked.

"It's an article about Prince Bertie's journals. They've been missing for over a hundred years! But it says here in today's paper that they have been found at Buckingham Palace. My . . . my . . . incredible. I looked everywhere for them when I was young because my grandfather told me that they contained the story of a lost family mystery, an Egyptian curse and an ancient cat."

Lupo's long black tail began to wag. It bumped

against the Duke's feet. The words "Buckingham Palace", "curse" and "ancient cat" heightened his doggy senses, sending them into overdrive. He scratched his left ear. It had been a while since his last adventure, but he'd never had one at Buckingham Palace and yearned to explore the mysterious royal residence with its many secretive trap doors, tunnels and staircases.

He bowed down at Prince George's little feet. "Buckingham Palace, George – did you hear that? Oh, if only Holly was here – it's been ages since I was at Kensington Palace. I do like visiting her there." Unable to hide his affections for the Queen's most loyal corgi, Lupo twisted on to his back and smiled, revealing his soft little teeth.

George *gooed* into Lupo's face, "Bucking-jam-Poo-lace!" They both fell into fits of giggles.

The Duchess yawned loudly whilst cradling her little baby. "A curse at Buckingham Palace? What's next? Secret tunnels underneath it?"

Lupo's ears pricked up in recognition. The Duchess couldn't have known how right she was. Lupo had known about the lost passages since he was a puppy. He had even used one of the passages known as Blue route to travel to Windsor Castle on one of his previous adventures. The Red route – which ran directly under Apartment 1A – remained unexplored by him. The short passage between Kensington Palace and Buckingham Palace had originally been designed as a tunnel for Queen Victoria but now it was used by ghosts and mice. It was sumptuously decorated and ran right under Buckingham Palace's tall brick walls and behind the royal police guards. Lupo knew it had been hundreds of years since any human had wandered through the passages.

Nanny appeared, offering to take the baby to give the Duchess a chance to finish making dinner.

I wonder what Holly is having for dinner? Lupo thought. One day, I hope I'll have a good excuse to use the Red route. Her Majesty's dogs stopped him from visiting Holly, and he dared not be caught using one of the secret entrances to Buckingham Palace by Monty, Willow or Candy. The royal corgis kept their distance whenever he was at their grand residence. When he visited with the Duke he would see them muttering in corners and turning their noses up at his relaxed, friendly spaniel gestures of goodwill. Vulcan, the Queen's dorgi, was far worse – he seemed to make it his mission in life to get Lupo into all sorts of trouble. Only Holly had welcomed him and helped him settle into his royal life.

Prince George was restless, so started pulling on Lupo's long black ears for attention. Distracted by thoughts of Holly, Lupo said, "The things Holly must see in that Palace, George!" He barked softly. "I'll bet she knows all about the lost treasures and forgotten mysteries!" His tail flicked happily in the air as a shudder of excitement tingled down his dark back and his long, tangled black ears twitched, eager for more of the Duke's story.

The Duchess saw the excitement in the royal spaniel's eyes. "The missing journal of an old prince? Sounds like a good story. I think you should tell George and Lupo all about Prince Bertie whilst I feed and change this little one."

Letting the paper flop over his large, comforting hands the Duke answered, "Good idea. Oh hang on, boys, before I begin . . . I will warn you that this story's ending is yet to be revealed. Perhaps now that the journals have been found, the mystery may finally be solved."

The Duke put down his newspaper. "Let's begin

at the beginning and worry about the curse, the ancient cat, and Buckingham Palace later," he said. "*This* story starts when Queen Victoria decided to send her eldest son, Prince Bertie, on an official tour of Egypt."

Lupo's heart began beating faster. He had learned about Queen Victoria and Egypt in his history lessons with Herbert, the smart brown mouse who was the Head of Mice Intelligence Section 5. He breathed in deeply and sniffed the big, yellowing globe at the far end of the room. The mere idea of the world beyond Kensington Palace filled him with a yearning to explore. As a young pup he and Herbert had spent entire lessons turning the globe, studying the different continents. Though he had never been there, he knew exactly where Egypt was.

Prince George whispered into the royal dog's big black ear, "*E-pit! Yippee!*"

Lupo replied in the secret language that only the two of them could understand – a language of *sniffs*, *chomps* and *licks*. *Sniffing* loudly through his wet, black nose, he said: "An ancient story!"

George settled as close as he could to Lupo's warm soft body and promptly stuck his thumb in his mouth. He curled his princely fingers around the spaniel's ears for comfort.

"Bertie was a very adventurous prince," said the Duke. "He was the first prince of England to do an official tour of the ancient world, its pyramids and the Valley of the Kings."

George asked Lupo what a pyramid was by blowing bubbles and *squirming* a lot. Lupo replied by licking the side of his face and *sniffing* loudly into his ear. "Herbert told me it was a big pile of old bricks," he said. George pointed to his Lego and Lupo nodded.

Patting Lupo's head, the Duke continued, "Oh and Bertie had a terrier, not a scruffy royal cocker spaniel like you!"

Lupo smiled proudly.

"Bertie left England on a royal ship," said the Duke. "It was a long and dangerous journey. To pass the time he read to his dog and learned all about ancient Egypt. He wrote daily in his incredible journals, which he planned to give to his mother on his return.

"Much to Bertie's and his dog's relief, they finally arrived in Egypt's hot and dusty capital, Cairo. The moon hung heavily on that first night. Whilst the

Egyptians huddled around a large fire and spoke of curses, the Prince lay awake, unable to sleep. He was too excited. In the morning the royal group would be leaving for the Pyramids, travelling by boat down the River Nile. They were headed for the Valley of the Kings!"

George stuck his finger in Lupo's ear and *mumbled*, "E-pit Kings!"

Lupo shook his head, dislodging the toddler's finger. "They weren't called kings back then. They were called pharaohs!"

George tried to stick his finger back in Lupo's ear, and *groaned*. "One day I will be a pharaoh and a king!" He pointed up to his father and giggled.

The Duke attempted to show them all how the ancient Egyptians walked. His long arms zigzagged together as he walked along with his knees bent.

"All the great pharaohs were found in the Valley of the Kings, George," he said. "They were buried in big tombs with the wealth of Egypt! But some of the pharaohs' tombs were protected by terrible curses."

Lupo growled playfully and George giggled as the Duke bashed his knee on a side table.

"Prince Bertie decided to take a sneak peek. He

scooped up his terrier, and snuck out of the camp in the dead of night."

George *waved* his little hands in the air and *grumbled*, "I want to go to E-pit with Lupo! I want to see the pyramids!"

Lupo *panted* and *scratched* at the floor, saying: "George, there are still lots of mummies in the pyramids! Can you imagine them trying to find a way out, fast asleep but walking around like zombies?"

George jumped up and down *gurgling* merrily. He reached out a wet thumb and both arms to the Duchess. She returned with the baby once again asleep in her arms. "Mummy!"

The Duchess bent down to George and kissed the top of his head. George waved at the sleeping baby and then put his thumb back in his mouth and resumed stroking Lupo's velvety nose.

"At the big pyramids, Bertie found a camel and headed out of the city and into the desert." The Duke waved his big hands across their faces. "Thick clouds covered the moon. Bertie watched as it totally disappeared! All of a sudden the air turned thick and there was a strange rumbling."

Mystified, the Duchess looked down at them.

"Bertie was surrounded by swirling sand. IT WAS A SANDSTORM!" explained the Duke.

George and Lupo both began *blowing* and *panting* as if they too were lost in the sandstorm.

"The sand was in his eyes and throat and covered his clothes. He needed to take shelter! The camel pushed through the storm, carrying the brave but fearful Bertie. Finally they came upon an entrance to a cave. Bertie and his dog crawled in, relieved to be out of the perilous storm.

"Inside the cave, they began to explore. They travelled deep into the heart of it. It was cold but fortunately the Prince was prepared and had enough matches on him to start a fire."

The Duchess excused herself, saying that supper needed her attention. Lupo and George didn't move a muscle. They had crawled under the oversized cream sofa, imagining they too were in a dark, ancient cave. Only their faces stuck out so that they could carry on watching the Duke. George *grumbled* and *blinked* several times in the darkness. Lupo moved closer, keeping the young heir warm, his tail resting on top of the prince's pink toes.

"This is the bit of the story I love the most,"

continued the Duke. "As the flames from the little fire grew, Bertie saw more clearly where he was. It wasn't a cave at all. He was in a tomb! Except this was no ordinary tomb. It wasn't a *human* tomb! The walls were covered in paintings of animals dancing, running and playing in the sunshine. Its floor was painted to look just like the sea!

Bertie sank lower to get a closer look. He saw fish made from silver darting amongst blue sapphire dolphins who were rolling in the water with stone whales. Bertie's terrier jumped on to the back of a giant turtle that was bobbing along the top. It was all so real that when the crafty dog tried to jump in and swim along he got a bit of a shock! When the Prince rested his hand on the head of a snapping green crocodile the little dog barked wildly!"

George stroked Lupo's nose. "SNAP! SNAP!" he *gurgled*.

"Flames from the fire flickered all around the walls and they lit up the paintings. Bertie saw tigers hiding in grasslands, stalking grey elephants which were rampaging through hand-drawn mountains. Below them were antelope, prancing in and out of a yellow meadow, and brown monkeys swinging on windblown trees!"

The Duke was pretending to investigate the cave but the living room was no match for the painted tomb. He said, "A door at the far end of the tomb was covered in hieroglyphics. It warned of a terrible curse."

Chomp, chomp, sniff said Lupo, totally overwhelmed. "OH NO, THE CURSE, GEORGE! *DON'T GO IN, BERTIE!* STOP!"

"Bertie pushed open the door to the inner sanctum, breaking the sacred seals!"

"NO!" said George, *gurgling* and Lupo barked.

"Bertie found himself in a room filled with ancient treasure . . . BUT!" the Duke cried, causing both Lupo and George to jump with fear under the sofa, "guarding the treasure were several sphinx statues surrounding a solid gold tomb belonging to a CAT!"

Lupo imagined the stone sphinxes arranged like George's toy soldiers. He made a low growl as his tail helicoptered round and round. He cocked his head to the left.

"George, I don't like the sound of this: Herbert once told me that sphinxes were the soldiers of Egypt's highest-born pharaohs. So it's odd that they would be protecting a cat! I don't think Herbert ever mentioned an animal tomb before? As for the curse . . . this really is a mystery."

George "meowed" – something he only ever normally did whenever he saw Kitty, the Kensington Palace tabby. "Pussy cat, pussy cat!"

The Duke looked down at his son who was gently stroking Lupo's fur. "Bertie was surprised to see that instead of a traditional ancient pharaoh death mask, there was a solid gold mask of a cat. It had to be a very important cat because it was wearing a pharaoh's crown and was clutching the sceptre and rattle that belonged to the ruler of Egypt. Bertie felt a chill on the back of his neck – he could feel the sphinx's stony eyes watching his every move."

George lifted up one of Lupo's paws and tried to hide underneath it, *grumbling*. "Hide!"

"Don't worry, buddy," said Lupo with a reassuring wink. "I'll protect you!"

The Duke leaned into the edge of the sofa. Lupo and George waited with baited breath.

"Bertie decided to open the cat's tomb."

Lupo looked wide eyed to George. "OH NO! Everyone knows you can't disturb a sleeping cat!"

Sensing danger he *barked furiously*.

"It's all right, Lupo," said the Duke. "Bertie wasn't afraid. Like you, he wasn't afraid of anything." The Duke suddenly grew more serious. "Something must have stopped him in his tracks. Maybe it was the ancient curse? Perhaps it was the hieroglyphics that warned of a terrible curse?"

George didn't understand what hieroglyphics were so he screwed up his face. The Duke tried to explain but it made George even more confused. So Lupo tried. He *wriggled* and *scratched*. "They're strange shapes of animals." He finished his description in a series of short whines whilst pointing at Prince George's Mother's Day picture on the mantelpiece. George *burbled* happily as he finally understood.

"You see, the tomb was cursed. Do you want to know what the curse said?" The two explorers under the sofa nodded slowly in silence, so the Duke explained: "HE WHO ENTERS, HE WHO WAKES ME, SHALL SUFFER THE CURSE OF A DREAMLESS SLEEP."

George stuck out his bottom lip and crawled out from under the sofa, wanting a cuddle from his daddy.

The Duchess returned to the room with Nanny cradling the baby. She handed her husband a glass of water. "Darling, you are getting everyone very wound up, right before we eat. Come on, Nanny, let's leave them to it. The lamb is nearly done but I might need your help with the potatoes if that's all right."

"I'm nearly finished," said the Duke, giving Prince George a big hug. "Bertie and his dog left the cave when the storm passed. Thirsty and tired, they finally got back to camp to a hero's welcome. Everyone was relieved to see Bertie safely back," said the Duke, glugging down the water.

Lupo *bounced* around, *yelping*, "Tell us about the curse! What happened to the CAT?" But it was no good – only George understood what the *panting*, *sniffing* and *whining* meant.

George responded by blowing a big round bubble with his spit, which meant he was hungry.

The Duke put down the empty glass, his thirst quenched. "Bertie returned to the cave with his servants and had all the treasure packed up and shipped back to England, in a box labelled 'Private, for Her Majesty the Queen's Eyes Only.'"

Seeing his son yawning, the Duke skipped to the

end of the story. "Now comes the mystery. The treasure was never seen again."

Lupo's ears lifted and he cocked his head to one side, thinking to himself, Now that really *is* a mystery.

"Some say that Queen Victoria was terrified of cats! When she read about the cat's curse she had all the boxes from the strange tomb thrown into the Thames! Others say she locked the entire contents of the tomb into a hidden room at Buckingham Palace. But no one has ever seen the strange cat's sarcophagus and her treasure was lost for good!" The Duke saw George's eyes growing more sleepy. "And what of the curse . . . ? Well, Bertie never slept properly ever again! His dreams were filled with visions of a deathly ancient cat."

With that, the Duke fell silent, as if lost in thought. But Lupo was transfixed.

The Duchess called out from the kitchen disturbing the uneasy peace. Lupo could smell the lovingly made supper, the Duke's favourite.

"I think that's enough," she said. "Bertie's adventures were a very long time ago." The Duke's stomach groaned. "Now, who's hungry?"